"I keep telling myself that it's over, that I'm safe. But I'm so afraid."

"What happened after he hit you?" Rafe asked.

Allie shook her head. "I don't know. I don't remember anything after that until I woke up on the kitchen floor. He had plenty of time to kill me, too." She lifted her gaze to meet Rafe's. "I don't know why I'm still alive."

Rafe's mouth tightened. "The fact you are tells me he knew for sure you didn't get a look at him."

"Which is fortunate for me. Not for your client if he's innocent."

Rafe stared at her.

Seven years ago, she hadn't known Rafe all that well. Still, Allie had been well aware that there had been something about Rafe Diaz, and it wasn't only his dark, go-to-hell looks. He'd exuded some sort of innate, brooding sexiness that seemed to promise endless nights of pleasure. Watching him now, she realized that hadn't changed.

Dear Reader,

Reconciliation. I have a soft spot for a story that brings characters back to someone they loved and lost. So, I thought, what about writing a connected trilogy of books about three couples with shared pasts? Stories where passion is intensified by memory and by deferred longing. And where better for lovers to come together again than in Reunion Square, an almost mystical enclave of quaint shops and businesses?

Three women. Three men from their pasts. Three different journeys that take us to the "ever after" part of love that was destined to be.

In the third of these books, lingerie shop owner Allie Fielding stumbles over the murdered body of a customer. To add to her shock, the private investigator who shows up to interview her is the man she helped send to prison. Hired by the slain woman's accused lover, exonerated P.I. Rafe Diaz believes his client is innocent. And though dealing with the woman whose testimony put him behind bars stirs up a past Rafe thought he'd dealt with long ago, it also unlocks a passion neither of them expected.

Suspensefully,

Maggie Price

MAGGIE PRICE

The Redemption of Rafe Diaz

Silhouette®
Romantic
SUSPENSE

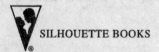

SILHOUETTE BOOKS

Recycling programs
for this product may
not exist in your area.

ISBN-13: 978-0-373-27619-6
ISBN-10:   0-373-27619-2

THE REDEMPTION OF RAFE DIAZ

Copyright © 2009 by Margaret Price

This edition published by arrangement with Harlequin Books S.A.

® and TM are trademarks of Harlequin Books S.A., used under license.
Trademarks indicated with ® are registered in the United States Patent
and Trademark Office, the Canadian Trade Marks Office and in other
countries.

Visit Silhouette Books at www.eHarlequin.com

Printed in U.S.A.

Books by Maggie Price

Silhouette Romantic Suspense

Prime Suspect #816
The Man She Almost Married #838
Most Wanted #948
On Dangerous Ground #989
Dangerous Liaisons #1043
Special Report #1045
  "Midnight Seduction"
Moment of Truth #1143
Sure Bet #1263
Hidden Agenda #1269
The Cradle Will Fall #1276
Shattered Vows #1335
Most Wanted Woman #1396
**Jackson's Woman* #1464
**The Passion of Sam Broussard* #1502
**The Redemption of Rafe Diaz* #1549

*Line of Duty
**Dates with Destiny

Silhouette Bombshell

Trigger Effect #47

The Coltons

Protecting Peggy

MAGGIE PRICE

Before embarking on a writing career, Maggie Price took a walk on the wild side and associated with people who carry guns. Fortunately they were cops, and Maggie's career as a crime analyst with the Oklahoma City Police Department has given her the background needed to write true-to-life police procedural romances which have won numerous accolades, including a nomination for the coveted RITA® Award.

Maggie is a recipient of a Golden Heart Award, a Career Achievement Award from *Romantic Times BOOKreviews,* a National Reader's Choice Award, and a Bookseller's Best Award, all in series romantic suspense. Readers are invited to contact Maggie at 416 N.W. 8th St., Oklahoma City, OK 73102-2604. Or on the Web at www.MaggiePrice.com.

For my girls, Roxie and Lexie.
Thank you for all the joy you add to my life.

Prologue

Annoyed, exhausted, Allie Fielding whipped her Jaguar into the driveway of the two-story condo in one of Oklahoma City's poshest neighborhoods. The dinner meeting she'd attended with board members of the investment empire she'd inherited had run late. She could have headed home after that, if only Mercedes McKenzie had shown up as scheduled when Allie closed her shop before the meeting.

I should *have gone home,* Allie thought as she studied the condo. She frowned when she found herself comparing its dark windows to sightless eyes. In reality, she knew that going home hadn't been an option. Not while she still had the hot pink garment bag that held the silk robe, red beaded bustier and two come-and-get-me sexy lace teddies she'd designed. The order had been rushed due to Mercedes's needing the lingerie before she and her lover left for Paris at midnight. Allie felt certain if she didn't drop off the items now, the long-legged redhead with a practiced pout would call, claiming some catastrophe had prevented her from showing up at Silk & Secrets, *and* from returning Allie's phone calls. Then she would wheedle Allie into making a delivery to the airport.

"No problem," Allie muttered. She was determined to prove herself in a career that had no ties to the Fielding empire her father had amassed. Some people might think Franklin Fielding had willed his fortune to his sole biological child out of love. Allie knew better. The idea of his money falling into the hands of someone with no Fielding blood coursing through their veins would have struck him as even more reprehensible than leaving it to the daughter he'd never wanted and had shunned.

As for the empire, her father's name was the one investors, board members and bankers related to, and his was the one they trusted. So she used it—grudgingly. Her own business, however, was her baby. She'd put all of her skill and experience and creativity into building it from the ground up. She would tend and nurture—and, yes, deliver items to the recalcitrant mistress of some wealthy man willing to buy her drawers full of lingerie.

But Mercedes had morphed into more than just a client, Allie reminded herself. The woman was dead-on savvy about fashion. At Allie's urging, Mercedes had begun designing the line of jeweled evening bags that were currently flying off the shop's shelves.

Allie climbed out of the Jag's cool comfort into the hot night air that was as dry as old bones. While she retrieved the garment bag off the Jag's backseat, the wind gusted, dragging strands of her blond hair from its sleek chignon.

The garment bag draped over one forearm, she headed up the drive, promising to treat herself to a glass of cold wine and a hot, frothy soak in sea salts as soon as she got home.

Although the neighborhood had private security patrols, she couldn't bring herself to abandon her one-of-a-kind designs on the front porch. So she continued toward the rear of the condo, the click of her heels echoing against the driveway, mixing with the sound of a car's engine thrumming to life.

Glancing over her shoulder, she caught the gleam of ruby-colored taillights as the car sped past.

She followed the lighted walk around the side of the condo to a patio furnished with iron tables and cushioned chairs. Overhead, tree branches swayed. In one corner of the patio, a fountain gurgled, its water bubbling into a brass sea shell. It was hard, in the middle of so much motion, to believe she was entirely alone.

The thought raised the hairs on the back of her neck. She skimmed her gaze across the patio. Then quickened her steps toward the back door.

There, Allie noted a dim light glowing behind one of the condo's closed shutters.

She draped the garment bag over a chair, then opened her purse. After jotting a message on a sticky note, she pressed it against one of the glass panes in the back door.

And gave a startled gasp when the door slowly swung open.

"Mercedes?" Allie stared into the dimly lit kitchen. In the shadows, just visible across the room, the refrigerator groaned, cycling through a new tray of ice cubes. The clatter as they fell into their bin was as startling as a gunshot.

Allie pressed a hand to her throat. Her pulse pumped.

"Get a grip," she whispered, even as the sudden sensation of being watched spread goose bumps over her skin. While the shiver worked down her spine, Allie caught something out of the corner of her eye.

She turned her head, looked down. Froze.

She was being stared at, all right, although it seemed the eyes watching her saw nothing.

Mercedes was sprawled inside the doorway, her well-toned body awkwardly turned on one side. Her pale face was propped on one outstretched arm as if she'd settled down for a lazy nap in the mint-green silk robe Allie had designed. But her eyes were open. Wide and unblinking.

Allie's body went numb. She stopped breathing but realized it only when black cobwebs began to encroach on her vision.

Reaching out, she gripped the edge of a counter and forced air in and out of her lungs. Had Mercedes slipped on the marble floor? Allie wondered as her gaze flicked to the four-inch stilettos strapped to Mercedes's feet. Fallen and hit her head? Did the blank stare signify death? Or could she just be unconscious?

The possibility the woman was alive propelled Allie forward.

"Mercedes?" Allie dropped to her knees. With trembling fingers, she nudged aside Mercedes's diamond bracelet and pressed her fingers against the inside of the woman's wrist, searching for a pulse. Allie felt no sign of life.

"Oh, God." Confirmation the woman was dead tightened the knots in Allie's stomach. Her blood pounded through her ears and she imagined she could hear the swish of it in her veins. Nine-one-one, she thought, her breath going shallow with the panic she felt closing in on her. She had to call 911.

Pushing herself up, she backed toward the open door while tugging her phone out of her purse.

The door's sudden swing toward her was her only warning she wasn't alone.

The heavy wood rammed against her shoulder. The force of the impact knocked the phone from her grasp and shoved her sideways.

A shriek rose up her throat when a dark form lunged from behind the door. She had less than a heartbeat to react before something hard slammed against her left temple.

The blow exploded stars behind her eyes. She landed hard on her side, the pain in her head a brilliant orange and red. Her breath shuddered in and out of her lungs while the marble floor seemed to tilt crazily beneath her.

Then everything went black and the world ceased to exist.

Chapter 1

Rafe Diaz's long stride took him swiftly across the grassy, tree-shaded area that formed the center of Oklahoma City's Reunion Square. He was a tall man, nearly six foot three, with a rangy disciplined build he'd honed to pure muscle during the years that others had control over his life. His slacks were black, his white dress shirt starched, the collar open. He'd bought his functional gray sports coat off the rack.

He strode past several boutiques, an antique shop and a bakery before halting on the sidewalk outside a wide display window that glinted in the morning sun. While he watched through the glass, the hot wind raked through his black hair like wild fingers. Rafe didn't notice. Not with his attention focused on the woman inside Silk & Secrets.

Allie Wentworth Fielding, heiress, socialite and party girl. Former centerfold model. College graduate. She was as stunning as he remembered, in a slim yellow business suit that managed to look both professional and feminine. The trio of gold chains draped around her neck added flash. A small, sparkling clip held back one side of her shoulder-length, honey-blond hair. Her eyes were laser blue and whispered of seduction from beneath thick lashes. Her skin was luminous, her lips glossed in warm coral that might make a man fantasize the heat was kindling for only him.

The sudden fire blazing through Rafe's blood had nothing to do with desire. It came from biting anger over how much had been stolen from him. Anger he didn't know he still harbored until his newest client had brought up Allie Fielding's name.

Seven years had passed since Rafe last laid eyes on her.

Seven years since he'd sat in a courtroom and listened to her testimony that had helped put him in prison for a crime he didn't commit.

He knew she'd told her version of the truth. Knew the evidence pointed to him. Still, he'd lost two years of his life and the chance to pin on a cop's badge—the only career he'd grown up wanting.

Curling his hands into fists, he shifted his gaze to the clock in the brick tower in the center of Reunion Square as it began to bong in slow, ponderous tones. Rafe counted the nine strikes while waiting for the resentment chewing at his insides to ease. He was free, dammit. Had been for five years. During that time he'd carved out a life for himself. It wasn't what he'd grown up envisioning, but it was enough.

He was his own boss. He lived alone. By his own design there was no one he had to answer to. For a man whose freedom had once been snatched away, having total control over every aspect of his life was all that mattered.

When he felt steadier, he turned his gaze back to the woman on the other side of the shop's window. He watched in silence while she arranged a pair of shoes on a velvet-draped pedestal positioned beneath a single spotlight. The shoes were embroidered and beaded, and looked like something Marie Antoinette would have worn.

Or a pampered, spoiled socialite with money to burn and country-club parties to attend.

While Allie positioned a small placard beside the shoes, Rafe focused on the dark bruise marring her left temple. Only a few days had passed since she'd found Mercedes McKenzie's body and gotten clubbed by the killer.

Standing beneath the strengthening sunlight, Rafe knew if he'd been gazing at any other woman, he'd be thinking about the fear that must have spiked into her when the killer lunged from behind the condo's kitchen door. And the pain she'd surely suffered when he slammed a fist against the side of her head. But this was Allie Fielding, and his foremost thought was that she could have wound up as dead as *he* had felt when she testified against him.

Rafe rolled his shoulders in a futile attempt to ease the tightness that had settled in them. He reminded himself he was here on business anchored in the present, not the past. There wasn't room for emotion, not when his client's freedom was on the line.

Rafe had already acknowledged the irony that *this* woman might hold the key to his latest case. He'd been hired by Hank Bishop, the man accused of Mercedes McKenzie's murder. Bishop swore he was innocent, and Rafe knew all too well that being accused of a crime had nothing to do with guilt. He was positive Hank Bishop was innocent, just as *he* had been.

"Get this over with," Rafe ground out as he headed toward the shop's beveled-glass door.

This time, he had no intention of allowing Allie Wentworth Fielding to play a part in robbing a guiltless man of his freedom.

Allie finished positioning a Plexiglas display cube over the shoes on the pedestal just as the chime at the shop's front door sounded. Her mouth curving to greet the morning's first customer, she gathered up her dust cloth, then looked across her shoulder.

And felt her heart clench.

Rafe Diaz.

She made herself turn slowly to face him. Emotion exploded through her. Each second seemed endless, drawn out, excruciating.

The same way it had felt in the courtroom during her testimony.

He was as tall as she remembered, but more muscular. Not even the gray sports coat could conceal shoulders that looked like he tossed around hundred-pound weights on a regular basis. His skin was the same burnished olive, but his face had changed. Hardened. Lines had scored into the corners of his eyes and mouth, giving him a taut aura of danger that hadn't been there before. Looking so dark and foreboding, he could pass for a bad guy. But Rafe Diaz had never been a bad guy, and Allie had spent years dealing with the pangs of conscience over the part she'd played in sending an innocent man to prison.

The cool disdain in his dark eyes sent the message he hadn't forgotten—or forgiven—her involvement, either.

Her fingers clenched on the dust cloth. "Rafe, what…
are you doing here?"

"Business."

Her gaze swept across the racks of silky lingerie and
shelves of feminine accessories. "You came to buy
something?"

"Hardly." He kept his gaze locked on hers as he
moved to the waist-high glass counter near the door.
"I'm here on my business, not yours." He pulled a card
out of the inside pocket of his sports coat, laid it on the
counter and waited.

The fact he hadn't walked to her and handed her the
card indicated he didn't intend to make their meeting
easy. Fine, Allie thought, as she moved toward the
counter, her heels echoing against the polished parquet
floor. After what he'd been through, she couldn't exactly
blame him for holding a grudge.

She stowed the cloth under the counter, then took in the
information on the card. "What business does a private investigator have with me?"

"Hank Bishop's my client. He's been charged with murdering Mercedes McKenzie."

"I heard he'd been arrested." Allie swallowed hard. She
hadn't yet been able to rid her mind of the vision of Mercedes lying dead on the condo's kitchen floor. "What has
Hank Bishop hired you to do?"

"Prove he's innocent."

"Do you believe he is?"

"I believe in giving him the benefit of the doubt." Rafe
dipped his head. "Not everyone who gets arrested is actually guilty."

Ouch. Allie felt heat flood into her cheeks. "No, they're

not." She laid the card aside. "You were innocent, Rafe. As much a victim as Nina was, but in a far different way."

Even after so many years, Allie still shuddered at the horrific memories. For the pain her best friend suffered. And what Rafe must have endured. "Does it make you feel better to hear me say you were innocent?"

She saw a shadow of emotion move in his eyes before the shutter came down. "What I want to hear from you are details. What happened when you found Mercedes McKenzie's body?"

Allie eased out a breath. Okay, so his coming here didn't include clearing the air about the past. Talking about finding a dead body wasn't high on her list of subject matter, either.

"I went over everything with the police," she said. "Several times."

"I'm not the police."

She hesitated when a long-ago memory stirred inside her. Nina, her best friend and roommate who'd been dating Rafe, had mentioned his driving goal was to be a cop. His conviction ended that dream. And though it had been expunged as if it had never happened, Allie didn't think any police department would hire a man who had served time in a state penitentiary.

"I want whoever killed Mercedes put away, so I'll tell you all I know about that night," she said quietly. "But I'm still a little unsteady from the experience. I'd prefer to talk over there."

His gaze tracked hers to the plush sitting area tucked into one corner of the shop's main showroom. "Fine."

When she moved past him, she caught the tang of masculine-scented soap. She had to stop herself from turning her head, inhaling deeply of the scent that was indescribably male.

As she walked across the shop, she was acutely aware of Rafe moving behind her.

Allie settled onto the powder-pink love seat. "You might as well get comfortable," she said, gesturing toward the upholstered chair on the opposite side of the round glass coffee table.

Instead of sitting, Rafe stood behind the chair. "About that night?" he prodded.

She leaned back against the love seat's cushions and met his waiting gaze. "All I saw was a dark form lunge from behind the door. I couldn't even tell if it was a man or a woman. I'm sure the police had reason to arrest Hank Bishop, but it wasn't because of anything I told them."

"He was arrested because he was Mercedes McKenzie's lover," Rafe said. "He owns the condo she lived in, his prints are all over everything, his DNA is on the sheets, he has clothes there. And he has no alibi for the time of the murder."

"So Bishop could have killed Mercedes and assaulted me."

"Could have, but didn't," Rafe said. "Do you know the exact time you got to the condo?"

"Right at nine-thirty. I paid attention to the time because I was miffed I had to deliver lingerie that Mercedes was supposed to have picked up here earlier."

"Did you see anyone else? A neighbor out smoking a cigarette? Someone walking a dog, maybe?"

"No."

"Did you hear anyone?"

"No," Allie said, then paused. "I heard a car start. And saw it speed by the driveway."

"Going which way?"

"East."

"What kind of car?"

"It was too dark to tell. All I saw were the taillights."

"How many?"

She blinked. "What?"

"How many taillights? What shape?"

She arched a brow. "The police didn't ask me such specific questions."

"I believe in being thorough."

You would have been a good cop, Allie thought and felt a wrench of regret for the unfair hand life had dealt him. "The taillights were round. Two on each side." She tried to picture something about the car during the few seconds she'd glanced its way. "I think they were high up, close to the lid of the trunk."

Rafe nodded. "You didn't see enough of your attacker to ID him. But did you get a sense of anything about him?"

"No, there wasn't time. Everything happened so fast. Too fast."

Before she could block it, the vision flashed in her head of the dark form lunging at her. The fear came barreling back, sending a wave of nausea lurching in her stomach. Leaning forward, Allie propped her forearms on her knees and shut her eyes against the blinding white spots spinning before them. God, would the image never start to fade?

"Are you all right?"

She flinched when Rafe's voice came from just beside her. She hadn't even heard him move. "I'm…fine." A sheen of clammy perspiration enveloped her entire body. "Fine."

"Fine, hell," Rafe muttered. With one hand, he shoved

her head between her knees. "You're as white as chalk and about to pass out. Take deep breaths."

With her head spinning and her vision dimming, Allie had no choice but to obey. *Please don't let me heave on his shoes,* she prayed as she dragged in a series of shaky breaths against the nausea churning in her stomach.

Keeping his hand pressed against her spine, Rafe lowered himself onto the arm of the love seat. Despite her dazed senses, Allie felt the pressure of each of his fingers through the fabric of her suit, all too aware of the latent strength in his touch.

"You have some water around here?" His voice had lost some of its hardness.

"There's...a small refrigerator off the fitting room," she said, keeping her eyes on the blurred toes of her yellow leather heels.

"Where's the fitting room?"

"Just beyond that arched doorway."

Without further comment, he rose and disappeared out of her line of sight, his footsteps hollow echoes as he headed across the shop.

Lord, Allie thought. How many times over the five years since his release had she thought about contacting him? Or writing him a letter to let him know how horribly sorry she was. In the end, she'd done nothing. There was no way to make up for the wrong that had been done to him. That she'd done.

Rafe returned, unscrewing the lid off a bottle of water.

Bracing herself, Allie eased upright and took the bottle from him with both hands. "Thanks."

She sipped slowly, concentrating on the simple act of swallowing the cool liquid.

When her vision came back into focus, she saw that Rafe had relocated behind the upholstered chair. "Feel like continuing?" he asked, his dark eyes measuring her.

"Yes." She lifted her free hand to her bruised temple, felt her fingertips tremble against her tender flesh. "I keep telling myself that it's over, that I'm safe. Then I see this blurry shadow careen from behind the door. I was so afraid."

"What happened after he hit you?"

"I don't know. I don't remember anything after that until I woke up on the kitchen floor." Allie squeezed her eyes shut. "The first thing I saw were Mercedes's dead eyes staring back at me." A shiver ran up Allie's spine and her voice broke. "I was unconscious for over half an hour. He had plenty of time to kill me, too." She took another shaky sip of water, then lifted her gaze to meet Rafe's. "I don't know why I'm still alive."

Rafe's mouth tightened. "The fact you are tells me he knew for sure you didn't get a look at him."

"Which is fortunate for me." Allie took another sip of water. "Not for your client if he's innocent."

Apparently assured she was no longer in danger of fainting, Rafe wandered past an array of display racks holding colorful, delicate silks. Allie noted that he moved with the sinuous tread of a big cat. No wasted motion, no abrupt movements.

Seven years ago, she hadn't known him all that well—he and Nina had dated only a short time. Still, Allie had been well aware that there had been something about Rafe Diaz, and it wasn't only his dark, go-to-hell looks. He'd exuded some sort of innate brooding sexiness that seemed to promise endless nights of pleasure. Watching him now, she realized that hadn't changed.

"Speaking of my client," he began. "Bishop told me that both his mistress and his wife shop here."

With her mouth having gone dry for an entirely different reason, Allie took another sip of water. "True, but I wasn't aware of that until after Hank's arrest. Mercedes made no secret she had a married lover, but she never told me his name."

"Who paid her bill?"

"She used a credit card in her own name."

"Did she and Bishop's wife ever cross paths here?"

"No. Mercedes always made a point to come here after regular business hours." Allie set the water bottle aside. "Look, I didn't pass judgment on Mercedes's lifestyle. But the fact is, she had a married lover, who apparently wanted her to feel free to buy whatever she wanted in my shop. I saw no reason not to accommodate the arrangement."

Rafe slid her a look. "And you wanted the profits."

His judgmental tone had Allie bristling. "I'd be a damn poor business owner if I didn't keep my eye on the bottom line," she shot back. "And you apparently didn't let Hank Bishop's questionable morals get in the way when you agreed to take him on as a client."

Rafe paused beside the velvet-covered pedestal to study the ornate shoes. "Point taken," he said after a moment.

Allie felt a rush of satisfaction at his admission.

"Does Bishop's wife shop here a lot?"

"Yes, Ellen's a regular customer."

"Did she know her husband had a mistress on the side?"

"If she did, she didn't tell me."

Allie's gaze followed Rafe's to the pedestal and the shoes that were to be auctioned at the upcoming benefit for the foundation she had established years ago. In the past, Ellen

Bishop had attended the auction, but now that her husband's affair was out in the open and he'd been charged with the murder of his mistress, Allie suspected it might be a while before Ellen was ready to show her face again in public.

"Bishop's partner in his real estate business is Guy Jones," Rafe said. "They're brothers-in-law. Bishop said Jones's wife and daughter shop here, too."

"That's right," Allie confirmed. "The daughter is getting married. I'm designing her trousseau. Neither Katie nor her mother have ever mentioned Mercedes in my presence."

Rafe turned, wandered toward a glass display case. "Do you have any other customers who had a connection to Mercedes?"

"Not directly."

"Indirectly?"

"The purses." Allie swept a hand toward the display case that held a number of jeweled evening clutches. "Mercedes designed those."

Frowning, Rafe stared down at the case. "She made purses?"

"She *designed* them. She had a savvy eye for fashion. When I saw her designs, I bought them. I have them made at the same off-site warehouse my seamstresses work out of."

"Interesting."

The sardonic tone that had settled in his voice had Allie narrowing her eyes. "Why is that interesting?"

"In college, you were too busy partying to bother attending class. Now, you oversee a financial empire and own this shop."

Irritation shot through her as she stared at his hard, emotionless face. Logic told her she should be able to shrug off his words. After all, what he'd said was true. She'd spent her time hooking up with wildly inappropriate boyfriends while thumbing her nose at her studies. Not because she hadn't been capable of making good grades but because it had irritated her father, and that had been important to her at the time. But a whole lot of life had gone on since she had last seen Rafe, and she was a very different person from the looking-for-a-good-time girl he had known.

Something inside of her that she couldn't define found it vitally important that he understand that.

"You're right, I sit on the board of my family's company," Allie said coolly. "And I've built my own separate business from the ground up. I'm about to start direct sales of the lingerie I design via my Web site. Things change, Rafe. People change. Sometimes for the better."

"Yeah." He gestured toward his business card she'd left on the counter. "If you remember anything else about Mercedes or the night you found her dead, give me a call."

Allie watched him turn, tracked his progress as he strode toward the door. And even though her muscles still felt like glass, she rose from the love seat. "Rafe."

He paused, turned back to face her, his eyes as dark and hard as flint. "What?"

"I'm sorry about what happened to you." Aware that her heartbeat was much too fast and labored for a woman standing still, she curled her fingers into her palms. "Truly sorry. I hope you know that all I did was tell the truth."

His gaze stayed locked on hers as an emotion she couldn't define flickered in his eyes. "You told what you *thought* was the truth. And I'm the one who paid for it."

Chapter 2

"Dammit, I don't care if Allie Fielding saw me at the condo. I didn't kill Mercedes!"

Rafe studied his client across the real estate developer's expansive desk. In his late fifties, Hank Bishop was powerfully built with black hair going gray at the temples and a strongly carved face with prominent planes. The stress of a murder charge hanging over him made those planes look glass-sharp.

"Miss Fielding didn't see you," Rafe said levelly. "She saw your car's taillights when you drove off."

Bishop dragged in a breath. "That should add muscle to my claim that I'm not the person who clubbed Allie in the head."

Bishop's comment shoved her image into Rafe's mind. Despite his best efforts not to, he pictured how she'd looked sitting on that pink love seat, her temple bruised, her cheeks colorless.

He'd left the shop hours ago and he was still fighting to shake off the awareness that had jolted through him when he pressed his palm against Allie's spine and nudged her forward. She'd been on the verge of passing out, yet the electricity that zipped into his fingers had been unmistakable. It was a connection he had not felt—had not wanted to feel—with another living soul over the past seven years.

The unexpected quake of emotion had pissed him off. He was still pissed off. He didn't need this, didn't want the memories spilling out, flashing in kaleidoscope tumbles, like the revolving red/blue lights on the police car that had driven him away from the life he'd once known.

"The killer had to have still been at the condo when I got there." Bishop bounced a fist against the arm of his chair. "Maybe when I went out the front door he headed toward the back, thinking he'd get out that way? Instead, he ran into Allie."

"That's probably what happened," Rafe agreed. "It's just that her seeing taillights matching your Ferrari goes a long way in placing you at the scene of the murder."

Bishop cursed. "My security chief recommended I hire you because you've got a reputation for digging up evidence that clears innocent people. That's what I need you to do for me, Diaz. Not tighten the noose that's already around my neck."

"Before I accepted your retainer, I explained it's possible that evidence doesn't exist."

"Dammit, it *has* to." Bishop jerked his tie loose, then flicked opened the top button on his starched shirt. "Mercedes was dead when I got to the condo. There has to be a way for me to get clear of this."

For a moment, Rafe said nothing. He had thought the same thing himself when his nightmare began. He'd been innocent, yet he'd wound up in prison.

"Let's go over what you told me about that night. See if we can come up with something."

Bishop eased out a breath. "Like I said, I arrived early to pick up Mercedes for our flight to Paris. I used my key to get in. She didn't answer when I called her name, so I figured she was upstairs. I knew something was wrong when I saw the stuff from her purse dumped out on the bedroom floor."

The mention of the purse sent Rafe's thoughts to the display at Silk & Secrets of the sequined purses the dead woman had designed.

"I found Mercedes in the kitchen." Emotion flickered over Bishop's face before he looked away. His fisted hand trembled. "I can't believe she's dead."

To give his client time to get a grip on his emotions, Rafe swept his gaze around the office. As on his first visit to the downtown high-rise, he could find nothing compelling about the cool black furniture and white walls. The place had the same stark feel as the cell where he'd spent two years of his life.

"The killer dumped out the contents of Mercedes's purse, so it sounds like he was after something she might carry around," Rafe said after a moment. "Any idea what that might be?"

"I have no clue."

"I found out the police discovered a state-of-the-art audio system in the condo. Did you have it installed?"

"No." Bishop frowned. "You mean, a stereo system?"

"The wiring was hooked to a recorder. Hidden microphones were in every room. Apparently, Mercedes used the system to record conversations."

Bishop scrubbed a hand over his jaw. "I don't know anything about that."

Rafe studied the man for a long beat. "Maybe you told her information about your business that could hurt it or you if it got out? She could have recorded all of your in-bed sessions with an eye on blackmailing you."

Bishop's mouth thinned. "If she did record them, it's news to me. And she never tried to blackmail me."

"Were you the only man she was sleeping with?"

"Yes. I bought her a car, clothes, jewelry. Put a roof over her head. I made it clear if I caught her messing around, our deal was over."

"Exactly what was your deal?"

Bishop shoved his chair back and rose. He stepped to the credenza, grabbed a crystal carafe and tumbler, then glanced over his shoulder. "Whiskey?"

"No, thanks." Rafe let the silence continue.

"Mercedes was a gorgeous, exciting woman," Bishop said. "She gave me something my wife and I haven't shared for many years. In return, I fulfilled Mercedes's needs."

"Which were?"

"Material. She grew up the kind of poor where you don't know where your next meal is coming from." Bishop took a long sip of whiskey. "As for blackmail, if she thought it would get her a nest egg, I can see her doing it."

"That's an angle I'll work on." As he rose, Rafe glanced toward the credenza, focusing on the framed photo of a dark-haired woman in her late forties. "I need to talk to your wife. She won't take my calls."

Bishop scowled. "Ellen doesn't know anything about this. She had no idea I was seeing Mercedes."

"How can you be sure?"

"I know Ellen. If she'd gotten wind of Mercedes, she wouldn't have kept quiet about her."

Rafe stepped closer to the desk. "You hired me to get you off the hook on a murder charge. The only way for me to do that is to find out who killed your mistress."

"Are you saying you think my wife did?"

"I think a man did the killing. Mercedes fought hard. It would have taken a lot of strength to overpower her. Same goes for the blow Allie Fielding took to her head."

"Then why do you need to talk to Ellen?"

"She could have hired it done."

"No." Bishop sat the tumbler on the desk with enough force to slosh whiskey over his hand. "She's not talking to me or you because she's irate and humiliated about the affair. Our grown son feels the same way. But neither of them would resort to murder."

"Speaking of your son, he hasn't returned my messages, either. Because he works here, I plan to stop by his office on my way out."

Bishop's mouth pressed into a thin line. "Don't waste your time. After my arrest, Will informed me he'll be out of the office a lot. Said he intends to spend time with his mother. That she needs his support now more than I do."

"Did Will know about your affair with Mercedes?"

"You think I'd tell my son about that?"

"I need to talk to him and your wife," Rafe said, ignoring the question. He'd worked enough divorce cases to know that secret affairs didn't stay that way forever. "Any idea how to do that?"

Bishop blew out a breath. "You wind up at the same social event with them." He moved back to his desk, shuffled through a pile of mail, then frowned.

Rafe waited while Bishop called his secretary. "Check with Guy to see if he's got his invitation for tomorrow night's benefit auction."

Bishop's partner, Guy Jones, was married to Bishop's sister, making the men brothers-in-law. In the light of Bishop's arrest for the murder of his mistress, Rafe figured gatherings of the Bishop/Jones clan might be tense for a while.

When Bishop hung up, Rafe asked, "Are you sure your wife will go out in public right now?"

"Positive," Bishop said. "Social contacts mean everything to Ellen. She isn't about to let anything I've done shame her into seclusion. She'll make sure everyone knows what a bastard I've been to her."

Both men looked across the office when the door swung inward. "Hank, you wanted to see this invite?"

"Yeah, Guy. Come in."

Rafe studied Guy Jones as he approached. He was short and burly, his dark hair thinning at the crown. His pleated khaki slacks, striped short-sleeved dress shirt and black brogans were a far cry from the tailored suit and polished Italian leather loafers worn by his partner.

"That's it," Bishop said, checking the invitation. He told his brother-in-law why he wanted it, then introduced Rafe.

Guy offered a hand. "Diaz, I hope to hell you can get Hank cleared of the murder charge."

"I'll do my best," Rafe said. The man's grip was like a can crusher.

The piece of heavy card stock Bishop handed Rafe was

an invitation to a silent auction. Rafe's gaze narrowed on the small pair of ornate shoes embossed on the card's upper center. He'd seen those embroidered, bejeweled shoes earlier on a velvet-covered pedestal at Silk & Secrets.

Rafe glanced up from the invitation. "The Friends Foundation. What does it do?"

"I'm not sure." Bishop flicked a hand as if batting away a cobweb. "Ellen and I receive piles of invitations and I never pay attention to the who and the what. I just sign the checks and she deals with the details."

Guy Jones shrugged. "Seems like Allie Fielding is somehow involved with this foundation. I know for sure you need more than the invitation to get in the door. You also have to have your name on the confirmed guest list. I can ask my wife to make some calls and try to get you in, but she's busy planning our daughter's wedding so I can't guarantee she'll get around to it."

"I'll get myself in." Rafe stabbed the invitation into the inside pocket of his suit coat. He needed to talk to Bishop's wife and son. Period. At this late date, the only way he could ensure getting into the auction was to use Allie Fielding's connections.

In his mind's eye, he pictured her cool, perfect face framed by silky blond hair, heard the echo of her sultry voice, and felt all over again something tighten inside him. It was that intense man-to-woman response that had kept his gut in knots since he walked out of her shop.

Then there was the memory of her faint, expensive perfume, which had been the best thing he'd smelled in years.

He shoved away the thought. Next time he saw her, he'd be prepared. Next time, he wouldn't allow her to get past the wall of control he'd built around himself.

* * *

Paint roller suspended in one hand, Allie narrowed her gaze across the small bedroom. "Rafe Diaz shut down an *entire* street gang?"

"Not single-handedly," Liz Scott replied while using a small brush to dab pale blue paint near the room's sole window. The pane was open, letting in a breeze heated by the bright morning sunshine.

"But Diaz got the ball rolling," Liz added. With her long coppery hair piled on top of her head, and the tube top and baggy overalls she wore, she in no way resembled the kick-ass cop she was.

"Wouldn't that have put Rafe in danger?"

"After spending two years in stir, taking on a street gang probably seemed like a walk in the park."

"I suppose so." Allie closed her eyes. Seeing Rafe yesterday had forced the sharp-edged guilt she'd harbored for years to the surface.

She opened her eyes when Claire Castle settled a hand on her arm.

"Having Rafe walk into your shop yesterday must have been a shock." The owner of the antique shop next door to Silk & Secrets had dressed for a day of voluntary labor in tattered jeans and a faded khaki shirt. The house they toiled in was being readied for a woman who'd escaped her abusive husband and had been living in a shelter with their kids. With help from the Friends Foundation, she was getting a fresh start.

"A total shock," Allie agreed, and squeezed Claire's hand.

One of the best things about having close girlfriends was knowing you could count on their support. Allie had opened her shop on the same day Claire finalized her purchase of Home Treasures. They'd met Liz that same night when she'd encountered them on the sidewalk outside their shops, drinking champagne toasts and attempting a tipsy ceremonial burning of a photo of the sexy federal agent Claire had walked away from.

After hearing Claire's tale of love gone bad, Liz torched the picture herself. Since then, the friendship among the three had flourished.

Now, Claire was married to the sexy Fed and Liz was engaged to a gorgeous detective, who'd transferred from the Shreveport PD to the Oklahoma City force.

In Allie's experience and twenty-seven years of observation, she had only ever witnessed love go bad, crash and burn. Seeing her friends genuinely happy in their relationships was an ongoing learning experience.

Turning back to the wall, Allie put more muscle into wielding the paint roller. "In fact, when I looked up and saw Rafe, I thought I was dreaming."

"When you called to tell me Diaz had shown up, you sounded more like you'd had a nightmare," Liz commented. "Which is why I checked him out."

"How did he manage to take down a gang?" Claire asked.

"He'd finished getting his college credits while in prison, so he had a degree in accounting when he was released," Liz replied. "His uncle owned a restaurant and needed a bookkeeper. Apparently he was uneasy about having his nephew do the job, but in the end he agreed."

Allie replenished the paint on her roller. "Why was the uncle uneasy? Because Rafe had been in prison?"

"No. The uncle was being forced by a street gang to launder drug money through his business in lieu of paying them for protection. It didn't take Rafe Diaz long to figure out what was going on. His uncle admitted the same thing was happening to other business owners in the area.

"Diaz got them all to agree to let him install surveillance equipment in their shops. Then he taped various gang members picking up payoffs. He took the recordings and the account books to the cops, and worked a deal to get immunity for the business owners on the money laundering. Between white-collar crime and the gang unit, they put away every member of the gang."

"Impressive," Claire said while positioning tape along the top of a baseboard.

"Word of mouth about what Diaz did was a boon to his PI business," Liz added.

"He wanted to be a cop," Allie said. "That's one of the things I remember about Rafe. His conviction ended that."

"But it was expunged, right?" Claire asked. "Doesn't that mean the slate was wiped clean?"

"That's what it's *supposed* to mean," Liz answered. "In truth, cops don't like ex-cons. There are some cops who'll always view Diaz as the guilty party, who caught a break and walked. That's not right nor fair, but it's the cold, hard truth."

"Which is totally wrong because none of what happened was Rafe's fault," Allie said, frustration honing her voice to an edge. "He was innocent. But the evidence the police had seemed to point to his guilt."

"What happened to Rafe was awful," Claire said.

"It sucks," Liz agreed. She stepped back and scowled at her work area. "So does my paint job. I'm sure there's some technique to this, but all I know how to do is slop the stuff on and wait for it to dry." She sent a look across her shoulder. "Al, why don't you just pronounce me a failure? Then I'll slink on home."

Glad for change to a lighter subject, Allie stepped across the room to get a close-up view of Liz's work.

"It looks fine to me," Allie said. "But if you think your painting's not up to par, I can transfer you to the scraping team. They're starting on the outside of the house after lunch."

Pursing her lips, Liz gave her work another considering look. Then she shook her head. "On second thought, I think I'm getting the hang of using this brush."

Rafe braked his car in front of a small house that had paint peeling off it like dead skin. Sawhorses sat on the porch. Frowning, he rechecked the card the clerk at Silk & Secrets had jotted the address on to verify he was at the right place.

He was.

The clerk had told him Miss Fielding was spending the day painting in the Paseo District. Because this area of the city catered to emerging artists and trendy galleries, Rafe figured he'd find her in an art class, sketching some nude male model, which would have been right up the alley of the sexy party girl he'd known in college.

He climbed out of his car just as a beefy workman wearing a sweat-stained T-shirt, jeans and a tool belt lashed beneath his bulging belly lugged a ladder from around the side of the house. Not quite the male model he'd envisioned, Rafe thought as he headed across the yard.

Moments later, he followed the workman's directions to the house's back bedroom. The smell of fresh paint hung heavy in the air.

At the bedroom's doorway he paused, taking in the lone woman working with her back to him. She was wearing an old, tattered pair of jeans with frayed hems. A rag stuck out of one of the back pockets. Her T-shirt looked as if it had once been beige but had been washed so often that it had faded to a soft cream. Her hair was stuffed up into a ball cap and her scuffed work boots were spattered with the same light blue paint she was rolling onto the wall.

"I'm looking for Allie Fielding."

At the sound of his voice she jolted and did a fast, twisting about-face. The momentum of the turn had her fumbling the roller, dripping paint on the floor.

She glanced down, then looked back at him, her blue eyes glinting. "You scared me to death!"

For a moment, all Rafe could do was stare while Allie abandoned the roller to the paint tray, then jerked the rag from her back pocket. Muttering, she crouched and began swiping blots of paint off the wood floor.

In college, the money vibe had rippled off her like heat—the designer clothes, "in" shades and foreign cars so sleek they gave the impression they belonged in a cage. Even yesterday she'd looked like the millions of dollars she was worth.

The woman presently crouched at his feet looked like she'd just come from Goodwill. And because her face was bare of concealing makeup, the bruise on her temple was the deep purple color of a plum gone bad.

The unexpected quake of empathy that shot through him settled like a stone in Rafe's gut. This particular woman had stirred enough emotion inside him for one lifetime.

"I didn't expect to find you doing manual labor," he said, the words sounding harder than he'd intended.

She flicked him a look from beneath her blond lashes. "*I* didn't expect to have someone scare me half to death for the second time this week."

Rafe's imagination conjured up the dark form that had

rushed out at her from behind the condo's kitchen door minutes after she'd stumbled on Mercedes McKenzie's body. He couldn't blame her for still feeling spooked.

"I'll make a point not to do that again," he said evenly.

"Appreciate it." She rose, tossed the rag on an area of the scarred wooden floor where newspapers had been spread.

Up close, he could see the ocean-blue facets of her eyes. Today, she smelled like soap. Just soap. A sharp kick of awareness left his solar plexus smarting.

Her eyes flicked over his starched shirt and slacks. "Something tells me you're not here to strap on a tool belt and get to work."

"No." He knew he should just tell her why he'd shown up, get business over with, then leave. Maybe then he could get rid of the hard, hot ball of emotion in his gut. But curiosity pushed at him. "What's going on with this house?"

"It's owned by a foundation. We're making it livable for a woman who got up the courage to leave her sorry husband. He thought she and their kids were his personal punching bags. All the labor is done by volunteers."

Rafe glanced around. "You doing the painting by yourself?"

"Two of my girlfriends are helping today. They left to pick up lunch for everyone."

"The foundation that owns this house," he said just as the high-pitched wail of power tools drifted in through the hallway. "Is it the same one that's sponsoring tonight's silent auction?"

"Yes." Using a finger, Allie inched the brim of her baseball cap higher. "Why?"

"Hank Bishop's wife and son may show up there. I need to talk to them."

Allie's eyes widened. "Are they suspects in Mercedes's murder?"

"At this point, everyone is."

"Can't you just go and see them?"

"I tried. They're both angry at my client over his affair and they have little interest in helping him right now."

"Do you blame them?"

"No. That doesn't change the fact that I need to talk to them. I understand I can't get into the auction unless my name is on the guest list at the door."

"That's right."

"I've been told you have a connection to the foundation."

"And you want me to get your name on the guest list so you can get in and corner Ellen and Will Bishop."

"Yes."

"The silent auction is a black-tie affair, Rafe. A lot of prominent people will be there."

In a fingersnap, cold hard tips of the anger he could never quite vanquish clawed through. "And an ex-con doesn't fit in with that crowd," he shot back.

She kept her gaze on his as color flooded into her cheeks. "That's not what I meant. Your conviction was overturned—"

"You think that fixed things?" He took an aggressive step toward her. "Want to take a look at my résumé? There's a two-year gap with nothing filled in. Makes it hard to explain when a prospective employer asks what I was up to during that time."

She flexed her fingers, then curled them into her palms. "I told you I was sorry. I'll tell you again—"

"I didn't come here for a damn apology."

Stepping away, he pulled back on every level. He stared

out the open window while the thud of hammers, the buzz of saws, the whir of drills coming from other areas of the house filled the air. Dammit, why the hell had he come here? He should have known that seeing Allie Fielding again would shove all the bitter memories to the surface.

"Rafe, if I could go back and erase that night, I would."

The unsteadiness in her voice had him looking back at her. She'd been an unwitting player in the event that had sent him to prison. She wasn't to blame, logically he knew that. Still, it didn't lessen the storm brewing inside him.

"What I was going to say," she continued, "is that the Friends Foundation depends partly on the donations made during the annual auction. If you confront Ellen Bishop or her son and cause a scene, some of the donors are bound to get upset. They might decide not to make a contribution. That will hurt the people the foundation was established to help."

Pulling in a breath, Rafe snapped control back in place. "I won't cause a scene," he ground out. "Most of the time I'll be observing. Reading body language. You have my word."

Allie's chin angled while those stunning blue eyes narrowed speculatively on his face. "Something tells me you'd rather have been boiled in oil than ask me for this favor."

"Make that any favor."

Mouth pursed, she jabbed her fingertips into the back pockets of her jeans. "I'll make a phone call and add your name to the guest list. But I want something in return."

"What?" His voice echoed the wariness he suddenly felt.

"We're behind schedule on getting this house finished. My girlfriends have conflicts so they can't work here next week. How about agreeing to put in eight hours of volunteer work?"

"I'm not much for painting."

Allie lifted a shoulder. "Pick some other job. When you work is up to you. Deal?"

Rafe glanced around the small bedroom. Thought about the abused woman and her kids whose home this would be. That, and the fact he could schedule his time when Allie wasn't around, clinched the deal. "Agreed."

"Great." She pulled a cell phone out of the front pocket of her baggy jeans. "Do you plan to bring anyone with you tonight?"

It took a moment for her meaning to sink in. "You mean, a date?"

"Yes. I'll have to add her name to the list, too."

Rafe wondered what she would say if she knew he'd designed his social life around a divorcee as adamant as he was about forming no emotional strings or connections. When they saw each other, it was solely for sating physical needs. Their sessions were dispassionate, verging on impersonal.

It was enough for a man who'd sworn to never again allow control of any aspect of his life to slide through his fingers.

"I'll be alone," he said.

"All right." She flipped open her phone, then lifted her gaze to meet his. "Anything else before I make the call?"

Rafe paused, taking her measure. The college girl he remembered had oozed sex appeal and dressed for trouble. He could find no resemblance between her and the woman standing before him in paint-spattered clothes. Yet, there was only one Allie Fielding.

While he watched, she raised a hand to brush back a wisp of hair. It was the most erotic gesture he'd ever seen, her fingertips brushing over that bruised cheek, her full mouth parting a little.

He shifted position, trying to shake off the disturbing sensation that settled between his shoulders. What was it about her that elicited emotion when for so many years he'd allowed nothing—and no one—to reach him?

"There's nothing else," he answered. "I got what I came for."

Whatever the pull he felt was, he wanted no part of it. He had his future mapped out. Allie Fielding was a part of his past.

And that was where he planned to leave her.

Chapter 3

The Friends Foundation's annual silent auction was held in whatever location seemed the most lavish, the most luxurious, the place best suited for over-the-top elegance. This year, a luxury downtown hotel had offered the use of its refurbished ballrooms for free, and the foundation's board jumped at the gift.

Although Allie had established the foundation, provided its initial funding and sat on the board of directors, she designated the members of the fund-raising committee to man the receiving line. That left her free to mingle and deal with any last-minute problems that might arise.

Tonight there were masses of people, delicious food on the buffet, ice sculptures, fountains flowing with chilled champagne and soft music overhead.

She moved from group to group to exchange pecks on the cheek and gripping handshakes. Some of the guests were friends, some customers of her shop, and all had made donations to the foundation in the past. Her goal tonight was to make sure they opened their checkbooks again.

She slid through the crowd with ease. Although she'd taken a chance wearing the red beaded gown with wire-thin straps when she had requested the hotel's air-conditioning system be set on full blast, the press of bodies heated the room and kept her comfortable.

Until she spotted Rafe Diaz stepping through the doorway. Clad in a midnight-black tuxedo, he looked large and solid. Totally gorgeous. His thick, pitch-dark hair was slicked back, his dark eyes stared out of the chiseled, golden-skinned face, scanning the room carefully.

Adonis should have looked so good.

While she watched him divert around the receiving line, heat welled in Allie's veins. Her heart pumped as though she'd just run a seven-minute mile. Her lungs tried to keep pace with her pulse, and her entire body was suddenly... *hot.*

No AC could cool her down now.

She had spent hours anticipating this encounter. And dreading it. Miss Manners had forgotten to cover the rules for how to best socialize with a man one had helped send to prison.

After taking a steadying sip of champagne, Allie began easing her way through the crowd to greet him.

Rafe paused just beyond the receiving line he'd avoided and surveyed the ballroom. It was huge and packed with people. Clad in tuxes and gowns shimmering with beads, pearls and sequins, the guests stood elbow to elbow under a dazzling trio of teardrop-shaped crystal chandeliers.

Enormous paintings in vivid, frenetic hues dotted the

ivory-toned walls. There was enough color in the ballroom to make Rafe's head swim. Yet through the crowd and the clashing tones, he saw Allie coming his way.

Her dress was a form-fitting glitter of flame with skinny, sparkling straps. As she moved, a side slit revealed a length of creamy thigh. Her honey-blond hair was clipped at the sides with something small and sparkling. Blood-red stones that he'd wager were real rubies fell in a rope from her earlobes to brush shoulders that looked as soft as her thigh. Her mouth and sky-high heels were the same hot color as the dress.

She looked, Rafe thought as his stomach muscles twisted, outrageously alluring.

When their eyes met, he didn't return her smile. He might not be able to control his damnable physical response to her, but he wasn't going to let her see it.

"Hello, Rafe."

"Allie."

She gestured toward a nearby waiter toting a tray filled with glasses. "Would you like something to drink?"

He flicked a look at the flute in her hand. "I'm here to work, not party."

"What a coincidence. I'm working, too."

Easing back one flap of his jacket, he slid a hand into his pocket and fisted his fingers. The scent she wore smelled like hot, smoldering sin. "Doing what?"

"Politely reminding the guests to slip into the adjoining ballroom where the auction items are on display. I stop short of making them swear to fill out bids. While I'm at it, I manage to squeeze in some wheedling for donations to the foundation."

"Wheedling," he repeated. "If you use the same tactics

you did when you got me to agree to work at the house for the abused woman and her kids, I'd say you're good at it."

"Very good." She lifted her chin, her red-glossed lips curving. "When it comes to acquiring donations, I'm known in wheedling circles all over the country."

With his eyes locked on her lush, compelling mouth, Rafe felt the hard jolt of desire, unbidden and unwanted.

Instantly he pulled himself back. Since the moment he walked out of prison, he'd made certain he controlled every aspect of his life. He had learned to block out the remembered clang of a cell door sliding shut behind him. To erase the black and cloying memories of having been caught in a living nightmare. And—most importantly—to strap back all thought and emotion that might threaten that control.

Now facing a woman who had everything inside him straining at its leash, he deliberately dredged up the hated images from his past, which included Allie Fielding sitting on the witness stand, testifying against him.

It didn't matter that he'd been free for five years. Didn't mean a damn thing that he'd carved out a life for himself. He would never forget the vicious helplessness that had ripped through him while he sat in that courtroom. Nor would he ever put himself in a situation where he wasn't positive he'd be the one pulling all the strings.

Like now. With her.

"Don't forget the party queen circles," he said, his voice a hard clip. "I imagine you're even more famous in those. Or should I say infamous?"

He watched with grim satisfaction as her blue eyes flashed, boring into him like a pair of cold lasers. If he couldn't trust himself to keep his distance, he could at least make sure he was the last man she'd want to be around.

Allie tightened her fingers on her glass. She understood why Rafe wasn't interested in letting bygones be bygones. Her testimony had been one reason he'd lost two years of his life. Still, she wasn't interested in spending time with a man who felt free to judge the woman she'd become based on past behavior.

"Since you're here to work, I won't take up any more of your time," she said coolly. "I haven't seen your client's wife and son yet. Perhaps you'd better wait by the door so you'll know if Ellen and Will Bishop actually show up."

"Allie!"

Pasting on a smile, Allie shifted in the direction of the female voice that had called her name.

Katie Jones, twentysomething and so painfully thin that her eyes looked like they'd been drawn by a cartoonist, rushed to Allie's side. "I about freaked when I heard you found my uncle's mistress dead. And then almost got killed yourself! It must have been awful."

"It was." Allie didn't have to glance across her shoulder to know that Rafe was still there. It was as if she could *sense* all the prickly intensity that seemed to simmer inside him. No doubt he had heard Katie's comment and decided to hang around to hear what Hank Bishop's niece had to say. Fine, she thought, angling her body back toward his. He was there to interview members of his client's family. The sooner Rafe did that, the quicker he would be gone.

"Katie Jones, this is Rafe Diaz," Allie said. "He's a private investigator, working to clear your uncle."

Pursing her mouth, Katie gave Rafe an appraising look. "According to my aunt, hiring you is a waste of time and money. She hasn't come out and said it, but I think she's convinced Uncle Hank is guilty."

"I hope to prove him innocent," Rafe said easily.

"Katie, how is your family?" Allie asked. "I'm sure this is a difficult time."

Katie nodded. "Aunt Ellen has flipped out. So has my mom. She's too upset to deal with all the stuff that needs to be done for my wedding. My dad said things at his and Uncle Hank's office are super-stressed." Tears welled in the young woman's huge eyes. "It's a terrible strain on everyone."

Allie gave the girl a hug, which was the equivalent of embracing a bag of bones. "Is your fiancé here tonight?"

"He and Will are getting drinks," Katie said, gesturing toward the far side of the ballroom. The movement sent light shooting off the gumdrop-size diamond on her ring finger. "Allie, will you be able to finish my trousseau?"

"Of course." Allie frowned. "There's no reason for you to worry about that."

The girl's face cleared. "I'll tell Mom. We didn't know how badly you were hurt."

In reflex, Allie lifted a hand to her temple. She'd covered the bruise with makeup, but she was still plagued by a leftover ache from the concussion.

"I'm fine. And I'm looking forward to your fitting next week." She patted the girl's painfully thin arm. "Your trousseau is going to be gorgeous. I promise."

Katie beamed. "I can't wait to try everything on." She glanced over her shoulder, waved to someone in the crowd. "I'd better get back to my family."

Frowning over the young woman's thinness, Allie watched Katie disappear through the throng of bodies.

"Something wrong?" Rafe asked.

She looked up. The intensity with which he studied her was unnerving. "No." She forced a polite smile. "Thanks to

Katie, you know that Will Bishop is at one of the bars, getting drinks." Allie took a step backward. "Because he's one of the two people you want to interview, I won't keep you."

"Careful," Rafe said at the same instant he gripped her elbow and nudged her sideways.

She glanced across her shoulder, realized she'd almost stepped in the path of a waiter balancing a tray brimming with flutes of champagne.

"Thank you," she said, conscious of the strength of the hand that gripped her elbow.

Their bodies were close enough to brush now, close enough for Rafe's warm, masculine scent to slide into her lungs. When she felt everything female inside of her respond, she took a step backward, forcing him to drop his hand.

"Even though you didn't come here because of the auction, you might want to bid on some of the items. In fact, there's an Art Nouveau lamp that's particularly interesting."

His expression remained unreadable. "I'll check it out."

"Good. I need to touch base with the staff overseeing the auction. Hopefully you'll be able to interview Ellen and Will Bishop while you're here."

"That's the plan."

She turned and walked away. And because she couldn't help herself, she settled her hand over the spot where Rafe's fingers had gripped her arm. She told herself it was just her imagination that her flesh still held the heat from his touch.

She had no hope, however, of discounting the fact that she was somehow far more aware of his touch than she'd ever been of any other man's.

* * *

Having studied photos of Will Bishop in the society pages, Rafe easily spotted his client's son among the attendees.

That done, he milled through the crowded ballroom, observing the young man. All the while, he felt himself being pulled, tugged at, by thoughts of Allie Fielding.

She was trouble. A smoldering package of temptation he in no way needed or wanted.

It rankled that there seemed to be various faces—bold, fragile, sexy, sensitive—of the woman he once believed shallow. Then there was the disconcerting knowledge that he'd spent the previous night with her face lodged in his dreams when he had worked so hard to erase that vicious wedge of his past she was a part of.

He shouldn't even be here, he admitted. If he'd given it some thought, he could have come up with some other way to question his client's son and wife. Allie Fielding was only a small part of the case, and he'd gotten all the information from her that he could. Instead, here he was, standing in a crowded ballroom, imagining he could still smell her sexy, compelling scent. He needed to get away from her—and stay away.

Forcing his focus back to his case, he watched Will Bishop step to one of the small bars set up around the outer edge of the ballroom. While he ordered a refill, Rafe studied his quarry.

Hank Bishop's son was in his late twenties, lanky and good-looking, with longish sun-streaked blond hair and a deeply tanned face. He wore an expensively cut tuxedo, but had left the collar of his crisp, pleated shirt unbuttoned and forgone the requisite bow tie.

Rafe had watched the young man work the crowd, moving from woman to woman, smiling and flirting while projecting an air of nonchalant cool. From the number of intimate female smiles and longing gazes he received, it was apparent Will Bishop had his laid-back Mr. Charm persona honed to a T.

If he was at all upset about his father having been arrested for murder, it didn't show.

Rafe stepped to the bar, positioning himself behind Bishop. When the younger man turned, gripping a tumbler of whiskey, Rafe stuck out his hand. "Will Bishop?"

"That's me."

"I'm Rafe Diaz. I'd like a word with you."

Bishop returned the handshake while Rafe watched his expression as he struggled to try to place him. After a moment, he frowned. "Do we know each other?"

"I'm a private investigator, hired by your father. I've been trying to reach you."

A flash of emotion tightened the skin around Bishop's eyes. Then his expression cleared. "Yeah, I got your messages."

"You didn't return them."

"Been busy."

"Doesn't look like you're tied up now." Rafe inclined his head toward the pair of tall doors he had discovered earlier which led to an outside terrace. "We can talk out there."

Bishop glanced toward the terrace, considered. "Okay. But I don't have a lot of time." He raised his glass, tossed back its contents, then set the tumbler on the bar. "Lead the way."

Outside, the intense heat of the summer day had lessened with nightfall. But the air now carried the scent of rain and was muggy enough that none of the other guests had ventured out onto the terrace illuminated by massive carriage lamps.

Will Bishop walked to the railing bordering the terrace, then turned. "I meant it when I said I've been busy. My mother freaked when she found out about my father's affair. And that he'd been arrested for killing his mistress."

"Your father claims he didn't murder Mercedes McKenzie."

"I hope to hell he didn't. But I'm sure wondering."

"Did you know about his relationship with the woman?"

"Do you really think my father would have told me he had a mistress?" Will shot back. "That he'd put her up in one of the properties he owns? Paid all of her expenses?"

"No," Rafe replied levelly. "I don't think your father would have told you about her. But family members stumble over information about each other all the time. So, I'll ask again, did you know about your father's affair with the McKenzie woman?"

"No."

"What about your mother? Did she know?"

In the glow of a carriage lamp, Bishop's eyes sparked. "She wouldn't have put up with it if she had. She's hurt. Going through hell. She told her attorney to draw up divorce papers. Which, because I can't remember a time when my parents weren't arguing and sniping at each other, is long overdue."

"You work in your father and uncle's real estate investment business?"

"That's right."

"What do you do?"

"I scout locations to see if they'd make good investments." His brow rose. "Dad thinks it'll build character if I start at ground zero and work my way up."

"Do you agree?"

"I think my dad should have paid attention to his own

character building. He created the mess he's in. There's nothing I can do to help him."

"Your father said you've been away from the office a lot."

"After what he put my mother through, she needs a lot of attention and support. She's my priority now. He and Uncle Guy can fire me if they want. At this point, I don't much care."

"Mind telling me where you were when the McKenzie woman was murdered?"

Bishop smirked. "Hell, yes, I mind. I told the police where I was. I don't have to tell you."

Will's cell phone rang and he pulled it out of his pocket. After murmuring a few words, he hung up and met Rafe's gaze. "I've got someone waiting for me inside. Any more questions?"

"That's it. For now."

Rafe stayed on the terrace, watching the young man stride away. When he pulled open the door to the ballroom, a tall, curvy redhead wearing a low-cut gown draped herself over his arm and gave him a pouty smile.

After Bishop stepped inside and closed the door, Rafe leaned a hip against the railing. Nothing Will Bishop said had put a blip on Rafe's radar screen. And his claim that his priority was taking care of his mother was commendable. Still, Bishop didn't fit the mold of a concerned son. Maybe that was because tonight he hadn't once looked his mother's way, much less spoken to her, during the entire time Rafe had spent observing him.

That, and the little twinge at the base of his spine, had him deciding to keep his eye on Will Bishop. And to find out where he'd been at the time of the murder.

Rafe checked his watch. Next on his agenda was to find Ellen Bishop and have a chat with his client's angry wife.

Striding across the terrace, he scowled when his thoughts returned to Allie. She'd done him a favor adding his name to the guest list. So he would track her down before he left. Thank her. Once that was done, he could head home, conscience clear.

After that, when he was away from her and his lungs were free of her intriguing scent, he would shove all thoughts of the woman out of his head.

But before he could stop himself, he pictured her face, her lush, red mouth. That long length of creamy thigh. He gritted his teeth while need rose inside him like a hot wave.

He was going to need a damn bulldozer to help do that shoving.

Chapter 4

Allie hovered in the hallway just outside the ballroom where the auction items were on display. To her relief, bids had been placed on all paintings, sculptures, trips and antiques. Even the monstrous Art Nouveau lamp that an eccentric matron willed to the foundation had snagged a bid. Not from Rafe Diaz, she noted cynically. And the pièce de résistance—the bejeweled, beaded shoes that had been on display in Silk & Secret's window for a month—fetched a dollar amount far higher than anticipated.

In all, a great night for the Friends Foundation, Allie thought, smiling. Then there was her annual pledge to match the auction proceeds. Tonight's receipts would buy several fixer-upper houses. After renovation, each would become a safe haven for a victim of violent crime.

For an instant, she allowed her mind to wander. She imagined if her father were still alive, he would be in attendance tonight. Not to show he was proud of her role in the foundation's success. As much as he had disliked her, Franklin Fielding had very much liked the accolades and attention of his society friends and business associates. The man, who'd purposely remained disconnected from his only child while going through a succession of wives as though they were water, would pretend a show of support solely for the sake of appearance.

At least he'd have been here, she thought. She couldn't say the same thing about her mother. At five, Allie had been such a burden to the woman that her mother had walked out and never come back.

When long-buried hurt scratched at her lungs, she eased out a slow breath. It was beyond her why she was wasting time thinking about the two people who'd shown her that no one came out of a relationship happy or unscathed.

Which was why she'd resolved long ago to put all of her time, energy and thoughts into her business. Her designs lasted. The people in her life rarely did.

When guests began streaming out of the ballroom, she flicked a discreet look at her diamond-encrusted watch. Handshakes were traded, air kisses exchanged. Although no major problems had arisen throughout the evening, she decided to hold off on breathing a sigh of relief until the winning bids were paid and all attendees had left the elegant hotel.

"You bitch!"

The voice coming from just behind her was so shrill it turned the heads of nearby guests and made Allie's throat go dry. She turned and felt her pulse bump when she saw the vicious anger in Ellen Bishop's face.

The woman was a trim and carefully turned-out forty-something with short, softly waved hair of dark brown around a sharp-featured face. Her mouth, wide and full, was painted coral. Her flowing emerald crepe pants and a silk blouse matched eyes that glinted with fury.

The smell of good scotch hovered around her like expensive perfume.

Considering that the woman's husband had been arrested for murdering his mistress—and word of the affair was the talk of the Bishops' social circle—Allie understood why Ellen had gone overboard on the scotch. But the reason for the seething anger aimed her way escaped Allie.

"Ellen," she said. "Perhaps we need to speak in private—"

"A little late for that. Everyone knows how you've made a fool of me."

Allie kept her expression benign, while willing her voice to remain steady. "I have no idea what you're talking about."

"Don't play innocent with me!" Gripping a half-full tumbler of whiskey in one hand and a crystal-encrusted evening bag in the other, the woman advanced forward two unsteady steps. "Are you even sorry about how you've treated me?" she demanded, her slurred voice turning venomous. "Do you feel *any* guilt at all?"

"Guilt?" Allie asked carefully. It didn't take an expert in human behavior to see that Ellen Bishop was as hot and high-pressured as a volcano ready to blow. The booze had apparently fueled the already-blazing fire, transforming it into an inferno. "What is it you think I should feel guilt over?"

"Like you don't know." With sarcasm dripping like acid from her voice, Ellen gestured with the tumbler, sending light flashing off her diamond bracelet. "You sold your sleazy goods to me while you did business with my husband's whore. You should be ashamed of yourself."

Allie raised a cautious hand. "Miss McKenzie didn't share personal information with me. I had no idea who she was seeing."

"You must have had a laugh, racking up sales to the wife and mistress of the same man," Ellen raged as if Allie hadn't spoken. "Did you design matching lingerie for both of us?"

Oh, God! Allie thought. The woman already looked like she wanted to cut out her heart—no way was she getting into a discussion of the lingerie preferences between the two women who'd been sleeping with Hank Bishop.

Allie flicked her gaze past Ellen's shoulder. The hallway was now crowded with guests who'd stopped to watch the woman's drunken tirade. At the center stood a bank president's trophy wife, best known for her insatiable love of gossip. It was surprising she didn't already have her cell phone plastered to one ear to give friends not in attendance the latest scoop. The woman reminded Allie of her fourth—and fifth—stepmothers.

"Answer me!" Ellen demanded with a drunk's bull-headed determination. "Did you design the same lingerie for both of us?"

Allie knew that when she sobered up, Ellen would no doubt be mortified over her behavior. But that was hours away and she needed to end the scene now.

Leaning in, she lowered her voice. "Ellen, the auction is over. It's time to go home. Let me find your son—"

Allie's words ended in a gasp when Ellen flicked her wrist and sent a river of scotch splashing across her face and chest.

"You have no shame!" Ellen railed. Fury throbbed redly

in her face as she raised her hand clutching the evening bag. "You even sold me one of the purses that whore designed. If it's the last thing I do, I'll see that you pay for making a fool of me."

"You're making a fool of yourself all on your own." The words ground between Allie's teeth as she used the back of her hand to blot scotch off her cheek. "You need to go home, Ellen. Sleep it off."

"Don't tell me what to do!" With the precise form of a major-league pitcher, the woman lobbed the crystal-encrusted bag in a line drive aimed at Allie's nose.

Swallowing a shriek, she ducked just as a hand swept in front of her face and caught the bag midair.

"Mrs. Bishop." Rafe positioned himself between Allie and the frothing woman. "I'm Rafe Diaz, a private investigator. I'd like to speak with you, if you have a free moment."

"Diaz." Ellen spat out his name as if it left a bad taste in her mouth. "You're the loser ex-con Hank hired to find some innocent person to blame the murder on."

Allie winced as a murmur swept through the crowd. She had to hold herself back from blurting out that Rafe had been a victim of a terrible injustice. That it was one she'd had a hand in squeezed at her heart.

"No," Rafe said while weighing the small purse in his palm. "Your husband hired me to prove he didn't kill Mercedes McKenzie."

"Go to hell!" Ellen's belligerent gaze jumped from Rafe to Allie. "Both of you. Take my bastard husband with you!"

Whirling around, Ellen expelled a hiccupping sob, then jerked a cell phone out of the pocket on her flowing crepe pants. Stabbing at buttons, she wove her way down the hallway.

Rafe shifted toward Allie, his dark gaze skimming down her, then up. "You all right?"

"I will be." Her hands were shaking so badly she curled them into fists. Taking a deep breath, she forced her mouth to curve upward, then turned toward the guests crowded into the hallway like sardines in a tin.

"When I promised the evening would be memorable, I didn't realize how true those words would turn out to be," she commented. While a few emotion-diffusing chuckles sounded, she accepted a fresh napkin from a waiter. "I want to thank each of you for supporting the Friends Foundation so generously," she added.

With the majority of the guests now heading toward the hotel's exits, Allie blotted the white linen napkin against the bodice of her whiskey-spattered gown.

"How about you?" she asked. "Are you okay?"

Rafe met her gaze, his compelling, olive-skinned face as calm as carved stone. "Why wouldn't I be?"

"Ellen's 'ex-con' remark."

"I am an ex-con."

"It was a mistake." Allie's fingers clenched against the napkin. "You were innocent."

"So what?" His mouth thinned. "That doesn't wipe out the fact I spent time locked in a cage like an animal."

Although they weren't touching, she could feel the tension in him, a live wire dancing with dangerous electricity. Allie searched for some words of comfort that might blunt the vicious memories, but she knew there were none.

So she changed the subject. "Did you walk up in time to hear Ellen accuse me of designing matching lingerie for her and Mercedes?"

Rafe nodded. "After viewing pictures of Mercedes and

seeing Ellen in the flesh, I imagine they had different tastes in more than just clothing."

"Good call. But if your client bought Ellen the bracelet with the heart-shaped diamonds she's wearing tonight, he didn't let their diverse taste stop him from giving them identical jewelry."

Rafe raised a dark brow. "Mercedes had the same bracelet?"

"Yes." Allie closed her eyes, remembering. "She had it on when I found her. I had to nudge it aside to check her pulse."

Just then, a man's voice boomed from the far end of the hallway. Allie turned and spotted Ellen Bishop's brother-in-law rushing toward them.

"I just heard what Ellen did." Guy Jones took in Allie's damp gown, mortification filling his eyes. "I apologize on Ellen's behalf."

"It's okay, Guy." Allie dabbed the napkin against her damp throat. "I'm sure Ellen is under an enormous amount of stress."

"Yeah." Jones shoved a hand through his thinning dark hair. "Ellen's not alone. I've got a daughter who's dieted herself down to a toothpick so she won't look fat for her wedding. My wife's going crazy planning the shindig. My brother-in-law and business partner is charged with murder, his wife has gone off the deep end and his son—my nephew—now hates him. To top things off, Will's ticked at me because he thinks I knew his dad was having the affair and I didn't do anything to stop it."

"Did you?" Rafe asked.

Guy's attention snapped to Rafe. "I wish to hell I had. Maybe then I could have talked some sense into Hank." Guy ground an oath between his teeth. "Diaz, tell me you're making progress on getting him off the hook on the murder charge. There's no way he killed that McKenzie woman. No way."

"I'm working on it." Rafe offered the crystal-covered clutch to Guy. "Your sister-in-law has one hell of a powerful throwing arm. She may look for this after she sobers up."

Guy's dark brows shot up. "Ellen *threw* this at you?"

"My face was her actual target," Allie answered. "Luckily, Rafe caught it. It's one of the evening bags in the line that Mercedes McKenzie designed. I sell them in my shop."

Guy stared down at the jeweled clutch nestled in his palm. "She made purses for you?"

"*Designed* them," Allie corrected. "Considering the circumstances, Ellen wasn't pleased to know she owned a Mercedes McKenzie creation."

"No wonder that set her off." Guy slipped the small bag into the pocket of his tux, then blew out a breath. "My wife and I need to get Ellen home. I'm sure that'll be just one more pleasant experience to top off the night."

Rafe pushed back the flap of his jacket and slid a hand in the pocket of his slacks. "I was under the impression her son is taking care of her."

"That'd be hard for Will to do right now, seeing how he's made himself scarce with some redhead."

Allie patted the man's arm. "I know you're dealing with a lot right now. I appreciate your supporting the foundation."

"It's all for a good cause." He forced a smile. "Not to mention a great tax write-off."

"There is that," Allie agreed.

She watched him turn. The way his shoulders hunched made his brawny body look as if he were supporting the weight of the world. Under the circumstances, she was sure that's how he felt.

She glanced up at Rafe. "I don't know about you, but hearing all that makes me very glad I'm not a member of the Bishop/Jones clan."

"Same here."

Rafe watched her blot the napkin against the elegant arch of her throat and tried not to think about all that damp, creamy skin. Or her hot, stirring scent that seemed almost erotic combined with the smell of expensive scotch.

Inside, his system rioted. Outside he felt rigid enough to break. It wasn't Ellen Bishop calling him an ex-con that had gotten to him, but the way Allie's blue eyes had glistened in anger *for* him. He didn't need her to jump to his defense. Nothing could change what had happened in the past.

Setting his jaw, he forced himself to focus on the vicious intent he'd seen spark in Ellen Bishop's eyes that had put his instincts on red alert.

He gestured toward the hallway the woman had disappeared into. "Is she capable of making good on her threat?" He heard the clipped hardness that had settled in his voice, but he couldn't help it. Allie was too damn distracting. Too damn...*everything*.

His tone sent a flicker of emotion through her blue eyes, but it disappeared before he could read it.

"Maybe. People still talk about the time at the country club when she hit the tennis pro with her racquet because he was late for their lesson. He had to get stitches."

Rafe nodded. A discreet check he'd run on his client's spouse had revealed she'd inherited a tidy trust fund. Having her own money would enable Ellen to hire someone to carry out her threats if she decided not to personally deliver payback. If she'd found out about her husband's affair, it was more than possible she'd directed her wrath Mercedes McKenzie's way.

Rafe gazed down at Allie and felt a sense of protectiveness that seemed almost foreign. He would have sworn that particular emotion had been scoured out of him in prison, where he'd learned to look out only for himself. That he felt concern for the safety of a woman who had helped turn his life into a nightmare was beyond ironic.

But felt it, he did. And he couldn't bring himself to ignore it.

"How many live-in servants do you have?" he asked. "And security people?"

"My housekeeper comes in during the day. The only security is an alarm system."

His brow furrowed. "Don't you live in your family's mansion?"

"No. After my father died, I donated it to the art league. It's now a museum. Why?"

"Where do you live?"

She arched a perfectly shaped blond brow. "In one of the Victorian boathouses on the Oklahoma River."

He had seen the neighborhood. Located on the section of river that sliced through the city's center, the gabled houses acted as a backdrop to the rowing clubs that sculled the water in shells and conducted colorful regattas. The residences were upscale and elegant, but definitely not mansions with the requisite high fences and security enhancements.

"Is there someone around who can protect you?"

"If you're asking if there's a man in my life who acts as backup to my alarm system, the answer is no." She went still, as a shadow of worry formed behind her eyes. "Wait a minute. Are you thinking it was more than just the scotch talking when Ellen made that threat?"

"I don't know. But why take a chance? How did you get here tonight?"

"I drove."

"I'll follow you home."

With a tilt of her head, Allie eyed him with so much unrestrained curiosity he felt the urge to shift his weight. "Why would you do that?"

Because he had no real answer, he asked, "Did you notice Ellen Bishop made a phone call seconds after she threatened you?"

"Yes."

"That call could have been to someone who could make good on her threat."

"Well, PI Diaz, when it comes to making a girl feel secure, you suck."

"I'm not trying to scare you. I want to make you aware."

"You've succeeded. Because finding Mercedes dead and getting knocked out by the killer is enough excitement to last me for a long time, I'll take you up on that offer to follow me home." She laid the napkin aside. "I need to slip into the ballroom and tie up a few loose ends with the head of the auction committee. I might be a while."

"Doesn't matter. I'll be here when you're ready to go."

Rafe would have liked to believe that his offer was all about her safety and had nothing to do with the heat coiling in his gut.

He knew better.

* * *

Nearly an hour later, Rafe followed Allie out of the hotel's elaborate main entrance into the heated summer night. The scent of rain hung heavy in the air.

"If you'll give me the valet ticket, I'll have your car brought around," he said, holding out his hand.

"I didn't use valet parking. I'm in the lot across the street." Beneath the bright lights of the arched portico, her eyes looked as blue as a tropical lake.

And just as inviting.

Control, he reminded himself. "I'm parked there, too."

As they walked side-by-side along a cobblestone path dotted on both sides by small landscape lights, Rafe's thoughts zipped to the past. This was the woman who used to rack up citations for parking in loading zones because they were closest to a shop's entrance.

"How come?" he asked as lightning flickered in the distance.

She sent him a sideways look. "How come, what?"

"Why didn't you use valet parking?"

"Let's just say I've learned the value of exercise." She lifted a shoulder, bare save for the skinny, glittering strap of her gown. "Besides, the parking attendants had a line of cars waiting when I arrived. I decided it was best to let those prime parking spots go to the auction guests."

"Who might not be as likely to bid on an item if they had to deal with the inconvenience of parking their own car," Rafe theorized. Out of habit, he swept his gaze up and down the street that ran in front of the hotel. This time of night, traffic was light. He noted several vehicles parked along the curb, the streetlights reflecting off their darkened windshields.

"Or not bid as high as they normally would because

they're miffed about the service," Allie added as they stepped into the parking lot that was illuminated by bright security lights. "The foundation depends on donations to operate. It's important that every aspect of the annual auction goes off without a hitch."

He watched her slide keys out of the beaded evening bag that matched her flame-red gown, then aim a remote at a hunter green Jaguar. The alarm chirped off and then locks disengaged with a muffled snick. She pulled the driver's door open, then turned to face him.

The breeze was just light enough to stir her scent. The three-quarter moon bright enough to emphasize the golden highlights in her blond hair. Need, dangerous and unwanted, clawed inside him.

"Speaking of 'hitches,'" she began, "I haven't told you how glad I am that you showed up during Ellen's tirade. She probably would have broken my nose with that evening clutch if you hadn't caught it."

Rafe thought about the strength it had taken to make the line drive that still had his palm smarting.

"She must pump iron to stay in shape."

"Clay, actually."

He furrowed his brow. "Clay?"

"Ellen is a professional potter. Once I did a fitting at her home for a robe she'd ordered. She gave me a tour of the studio Hank added on to their poolhouse. She even showed me how to form a bowl."

"I've heard that potting takes a lot of manual labor."

"It does. Just seeing Ellen pick up a mound of clay, then throw it around, beat it, twist and turn it left me exhausted. I remember thinking how great a workout she was getting." Allie gave him a sardonic look. "Seems I was right."

"A few years of that, anyone is bound to have arms and hands like a wrestler."

"I suppose."

"Suppose this. During your confrontation tonight, Ellen Bishop exhibited the characteristics of a pit bull. That's undeniable proof she has a violent streak. Mercedes McKenzie fought her attacker. Hard. Whoever strangled her and clubbed you in the head was strong."

Eyes going wide, Allie regarded him in dismay. "Do you honestly think Ellen is the killer?"

"If she found out her husband had moved his mistress into a condo, paid all of her expenses and was about to fly her to Paris, I don't think she would have ignored it."

"You're right," Allie agreed. "She would have felt threatened. Insulted."

"She needs to be checked out."

"Wouldn't the police have already done that?"

"Should have. I prefer to find out for myself if she has an alibi for the time of the murder. If she does, it needs to be verified to see if she really was where she claimed to be. Even then that won't prove her innocent."

"Why not?"

"She has her own trust fund and doesn't have to explain to anyone how she spends the money. She could have hired someone to strangle her husband's mistress."

"Thanks to you, I've gone from viewing Ellen as the humiliated wronged wife to a possible killer."

"*Possible* being the key word."

Allie nodded slowly. "When you talk about this case, you sound like a cop. I remember you always wanted to be one."

His jaw went rigid. "Ancient history."

"Not so ancient that it isn't hanging between us," she

countered. "Rafe, if you were any other man, I'd think you were being gallant to follow me home. But that's not the case. We share an unpleasant past. You didn't like me then, and I get the impression you think very little of me now. I can't help but wonder why you're bothering to go out of your way for me."

"You need someone to watch your back. I'm available. Nothing more."

"Nothing more," she murmured while reaching up to straighten his black bow tie. "All right, then." She hesitated, her fingers brushing the black silk. "I'd like it some day if we could be friends."

"Friends," he repeated. He could almost feel the warmth from her fingers as she adjusted his tie. His lungs went tight. He didn't want her touching him, not when her scent already had him precariously perched on the edge.

"*Cautious* friends," she suggested at the same instant the tip of one of her fingers skimmed his jaw.

Heat. It was as instantaneous as the flare of a match, jumping from her flesh to his. His hand shot out, locked on her wrist. The jolting move brought her a teetering step forward.

"Be careful," he said.

Her face was close to his now, their bodies just touching. With the sultry summer night and something even more sweltering between them, he fought the raw need twisting inside him.

Let her go.

Somewhere in the back of his mind, the order nudged him. But instead of nudging her away, his wayward fingers tightened, drawing her closer.

"Be careful of what?" Her voice had gone as low and steamy as the air around them.

She was soft, the kind of soft that blew a man's good intentions straight to hell. Her scent made his head spin. If she'd been a drug, she'd be wearing a warning label. And like a junkie desperate for his next fix, all he could think of was tasting her, drawing her in.

Oblivious to everything but the feel of her silky skin under his hand, it took a moment to register the distant pulsing of an engine, then the squeal of tires.

Rafe jerked his head sideways, spotted the single headlight heading in their direction. Adrenaline and instinct taking over with a kick as quick and hard as a mule's, he shoved Allie behind him, shielding her body with his.

A helmeted driver on a black motorcycle pulled to the curb. He glanced their way while revving the engine. The motorcycle did a U-turn, its back wheel skidding sideways. Then it righted, zooming off in the direction it had come from.

"Do you think that rider had anything to do with Ellen's threat?" Allie asked from behind him.

"I don't know." Eyes narrowed, he tried to read the motorcycle's tag, but the light over it was either burned out or had been removed. He kept his gaze on the single red taillight until it disappeared around a distant corner.

He shifted a step back. "It could have been some teenager out joyriding. Or some guy on his way to pick up a pack of cigarettes."

"True. Guess I'm being paranoid."

His gaze dropped to her glossed lips. Before the motorcycle showed up, he'd been close to kissing her. That knowledge had his gut clenching. He'd spent years rebuilding his life, fighting to take back the control that had been stolen from him. And here was this woman who was poised to make a mockery of that control.

Which was something he would not allow.

"Rafe?"

His gaze jerked to meet hers. He saw an awareness in her eyes that had him wondering if she had read his thoughts.

No matter who the man was on the motorcycle, Rafe figured he owed him thanks for preventing what would have been a huge mistake on his part.

"What?" *Cool off,* he told himself. *Focus.*

As if on cue, a light mist began to fall.

She flicked a look at the dark sky. "We'd better go."

Nodding, he stepped back, pulling open wider the door of her Jaguar. "I'll be right behind you," he said.

And he would stay there, he told himself even as desire ribboned through him, as warm as a fever in his blood.

Far behind.

Chapter 5

The ringing phone dragged Allie out of a restless sleep.

Rafe, she thought as she fought to free her legs from the twisted sheet. She'd been dreaming about Rafe. A hot, lusty dream. One that seemed so real that finding herself in an empty bed sent a river of hot, frustrated need rippling through her.

The phone trilled again, jerking her fully awake.

A weak, muffled roll of thunder sounded in the distance as she leaned toward the nightstand. The storm that had set in while she drove home from the silent auction was moving on.

She snatched up the receiver at the same time she caught a glimpse of the glowing red numbers on her alarm clock. Who the hell was calling at 3:04 a.m.?

"Hello?" she muttered, dropping her head back onto her pillow.

"Is this Allie Fielding?"

She struggled to place the deep male voice. "Yes. Who's this?"

"Detective Young. Ma'am, I'm calling about your warehouse. There's been a break-in."

"Oh, no!" Allie closed her eyes. All of the shop's extra stock was stored there, many of her original designs, the layouts for the catalog that would soon be mailed in conjunction with the launch of her retail Web site. The one-of-a-kind trousseaus in various stages for three brides-to-be.

"I need you to meet me here so you can do an inventory for stolen items," the detective added.

"All right." She stabbed her fingers through her tangled hair, shoving it away from her face. "My warehouse is equipped with a new state-of-the-art alarm. How did the burglar get in?"

"Kicked open a door."

"But, the alarm—"

"Ma'am, if you could just get here as soon as possible, I'll answer as many of your questions as I can." His voice had shifted into a flat police speak, the same tone Allie had heard Liz use when she went into cop mode.

"Of course." Allie kicked off the sheet and climbed out of her pine sleigh bed. Anchoring the phone between her shoulder and chin, her fingers went to work on the small pearl buttons on her filmy peach teddy.

"I…can you at least tell me if the burglar got into the safe, Detective…?" She furrowed her forehead as she headed toward her walk-in closet. "I'm sorry, you woke me up out of a sound sleep. What did you say your name is?"

"Young. The safe wasn't breached."

"That's a relief."

"One thing, if you have a list of serial numbers for the office equipment you had here, it'd help if you could bring it. I'll need the information for my report."

Allie's fingers went still on the buttons. The office equipment she'd *had* there? Her stomach dropped to her bare feet and her toes curled into the plush coral carpet. Holy hell, what all had the burglar stolen?

Telling herself she would find out soon enough, she eased out a resigned breath. Everything was insured. *Heavily.*

"I have the serial numbers on my computer. I'll print the information and have it with me when I meet you."

"Good. Hold on a minute."

Across the line, Allie heard what sounded like the muted voice of a police dispatcher.

A second later, the detective said, "A call just went out on a burglary in progress at a nearby warehouse. I need to answer that. If I get tied up there, I'll send another officer to meet you here at your place."

"All right." Allie stepped into her walk-in closet and grabbed the nearest pair of starched jeans. "I should be there in about twenty minutes."

"Drive carefully."

Surveillance was easy enough, Rafe thought. All you had to do was stay out of sight and watch. During the five years he'd been a PI, he had conducted uncountable hours of surveillance. Tonight, as always, the greatest enemy was boredom.

While a rumble of thunder sounded the storm's retreat, he checked his watch for the hundredth time since he'd parked in a spot that gave him a prime view of Allie Fielding's three-story boathouse. He scowled when he saw that only two minutes had passed since he'd last checked the time.

It had already been a long night. And it wasn't over yet.

If anyone had asked why he'd set up a stakeout in the upper-class neighborhood where the river edged manicured backyards that boasted architect-designed boat docks, he'd have claimed he was there on business.

There was, after all, a measure of truth to that.

Earlier, he had witnessed the wife of one of his clients in major meltdown-mode. If the phone call Ellen Bishop made after threatening Allie had been to the same person she'd hired to kill her husband's mistress—*if* she'd had the mistress killed—then said killer might possibly show up at Allie's house to make good on the threat. If that happened, Rafe was in place to take down the suspect and clear his client of the murder charge.

A lot of "ifs," Rafe thought, scrubbing a palm over his stubbled jaw. But for a man who in no way wanted to admit, even to himself, that the main reason he was there was to protect a certain blue-eyed blonde, those "ifs" would have to do.

She had no idea he was watching her house. And he didn't intend for her to find out because it was a niggling in his gut, not any kind of hard evidence, that had kept him in the area after he followed her home from the silent auction. Unless something unforeseen happened on the case, he had no reason to see the woman again. No reason to try to figure out the enigma that the once society wild child had become in his mind.

No reason to even *think* about her.

That suited him. He needed to focus on business. Period. Although he was currently running investigations for a handful of clients, his most urgent case was Hank Bishop's. The real estate developer had hired a cunning defense attorney, whose scorched earth tactics were legendary. But not even the best lawyer in the world could get Bishop a win in court if no evidence came to light to clear him.

"My job to find it," Rafe muttered, then took a sip of the coffee he'd bought at the trendy convenience store that sat at the only entrance to the upscale neighborhood.

Air cooled by the recent rainstorm wafted through the car's open windows while his gaze focused on the set of French doors just off the boathouse's second-floor balcony. Light had flicked off behind those now-darkened panes several hours ago. Allie's bedroom, he figured. What kind of sheets did a woman who smelled like all kinds of sin and designed sexy lingerie for a living sleep on? More to the point, what did she sleep *in?* One of the barely there pieces of silk he'd spotted on the one visit he'd made to her shop? Or nothing at all?

Remembering the feel of her soft flesh, he felt himself stir.

"Dammit," he grated. He should just leave. Head for the 24/7 gym he belonged to, and pump iron until he forced her scent out of his lungs, and thoughts of her out of his head. Then he would head home, climb into bed and fall into a dead sleep.

He scrubbed a hand over his face. Having Allie Fielding lodged in his brain wasn't the only thing with the power to disturb his sleep, he reminded himself. There was prison, too.

After five years of freedom, the nightmarish images that had jolted him awake night after night in his cell should be a faded memory. But they still had the power to rip him out of sleep with razor-sharp talons, the heavy stench of days-old sweat and perpetual fear plunging him back into that living hellhole.

The dream came too often for comfort.

Yet it served as a reminder that when a man let the reins slip from his control, he was vulnerable. So whatever it was that had sizzled inside him for that one fleeting moment when he stood inches from Allie in that hotel parking lot, had to be held in check.

He would see to it.

Clenching and unclenching his fist, he kept his gaze on her boathouse while sipping his coffee. And tried not to think about how shallow his breathing had gone.

Suddenly, light flicked on behind the upstairs French doors.

Rafe plunked the coffee cup into the car's holder and leaned forward.

Minutes later, a second upstairs light came on. Then both went out. He waited, watching, and saw a light turn on behind one of the downstairs windows.

Rafe knew her going downstairs could be something as innocuous as a raid on the refrigerator. Still it was possible a noise outside had dragged her out of bed.

Either way, he needed to check.

Having long ago disabled his Mustang's dome light, he eased out of the door, closing it behind him with an inaudible click. Earlier, he'd traded his tuxedo for the black jeans and long-sleeved T-shirt he kept in the trunk. If he stayed in the shadows, there was little chance he'd be spotted.

He had just crossed the street and stepped into the boathouse's front yard when the glare of headlights licked around from its rear. He crouched, using a shrub to shield his presence as the car appeared down the sloped driveway. In the illumination from a nearby streetlamp, he saw it was Allie's Jaguar.

He had no idea where she was headed at this time of night. Morning, he corrected, glancing again at the luminous dial of his watch.

He rose slowly while his gaze tracked the Jag's progress down the street. At the first corner it came to, its brake lights flashed on, spearing the darkness briefly before it turned.

He took in some air and let it out slowly with his lips pursed in a kind of silent whistle. The Allie Fielding of seven years ago had come and gone from the apartment she shared with her roommate at all times of the day and night. So maybe she had a late date. Or an early one.

Hell, maybe everything was fine and she was headed to the grocery store to pick up some Rocky Road. Following her might be a waste of time.

Problem was, a disturbing sensation in his gut had his instincts clanging like a fire alarm.

With every protective instinct rearing up inside him, Rafe jogged back to his Mustang.

Rafe had Allie's car in sight by the time it turned out of the exclusive housing addition and headed south.

He had just stopped at the intersection, preparing to make the same turn when a dark car parked on a side road switched on its headlights and pulled in behind her. There was enough illumination from a streetlight for Rafe to tell that the car was a maroon Crown Vic. Its male driver appeared to be alone.

For no other reason than his gut told him to, he switched off his car's headlights, counted to ten, then turned onto the street. The road had few lights and he made sure to stay far enough back that, unless its driver watched for a tail, there was little chance he'd spot the black Mustang.

And little chance Allie would notice the Crown Vic, because it varied its speed. Once it even dropped back far enough to allow a pickup truck bearing the logo of the city's newspaper to turn in between them.

Because he was too far away to read the tag, Rafe grabbed his digital camera off the passenger seat. Through its powerful lens, he discovered the car's tag had been smeared with mud, rendering it unreadable.

There was no mud anywhere else on the car's rear. Meaning, the tag had been purposely obscured.

Why?

Fifteen minutes later, the three-car entourage reached a dingy area of the city's southside that sprouted warehouses and a few small manufacturing facilities. Up ahead, Allie's car topped a rise, then slowed. The street, still covered with a wet sheen from the rain, reflected the Jag's brake lights.

And the Crown Vic's.

If Rafe had any remaining doubts that she was being tailed, they ended when the car followed hers into what looked like a mini city of warehouses.

He thought back to the interview he'd conducted with Allie at Silk & Secrets. She'd mentioned having an off-site warehouse that her seamstresses worked out of. That warehouse was probably in this complex, Rafe reasoned. He supposed the guy behind Allie could be a business contact who'd arranged to follow her there for some legitimate purpose.

But why so early in the morning? And why with mud smeared on his car tag?

Rafe set his jaw. If he'd had Allie's cell-phone number, he would call and ask if she knew the guy behind her. But he didn't know the number. Hadn't had a reason to ask for it.

Up ahead, the Jaguar turned into a parking area. Instead of following, the vehicle behind hers slowed, then braked against a curb.

If the driver was supposed to have been following her, why not just turn in behind her?

A warning blared in Rafe's brain. Allie didn't know she'd been tailed.

With his car's headlights still off, Rafe whipped a quick turn up a side street lined by another grouping of warehouses. He parked out of the light-spill from the night spots in metal cages mounted on the corner of each warehouse. He pulled his automatic out of the console, checked to make sure it was loaded. It was. He grabbed the flashlight he kept under the seat, then eased out of the door.

Grateful now that he'd dressed all in black, he retraced his route, then eased around the corner. The Crown Vic hadn't moved from the curb. Its idling engine was a soft hum in the still night air.

Keeping low, Rafe headed toward the car at an angle, making sure his reflection couldn't get picked up in any of the car's mirrors. Closer now, he verified the driver was alone. From where the guy sat, he had a clear view of the lot where the Jaguar was now parked.

In his peripheral vision, Rafe saw Allie get out of her car. Hoisting a tote bag over one shoulder, she headed to a warehouse's lighted door.

Rafe felt his gut tighten while he watched the driver's head move slowly, tracking her progress.

If he'd harbored any doubt the guy was watching her, it was gone.

Keys in hand, Allie stood in a pool of light at the locked door of her warehouse, trying to make sense of the fact the alarm panel showed the system was activated. She might have been in the throes of a hot dream about Rafe Diaz when Detective Young called, but she'd been wide-awake by the time he told her some burglar had kicked in the door.

Standing there alone in the dead of night, she began to have a very bad feeling.

She dragged in a deep breath in an attempt to control the adrenaline gushing through her system. There had to be a logical explanation, she reasoned. It would be nice if Detective Young were here to give her one. Or the police officer he assured her would meet her in his absence.

Because that bad feeling was getting worse by the minute, she decided to call a cop she knew—Liz Scott.

Holding the automatic hidden behind one thigh, Rafe sidled from the rear of the car, stopping just behind the driver's door. Clicking on the flashlight, he trained the beam through the open window at an angle that would blind the guy.

"How's it going, pal?"

His quarry jolted, jerked his head sideways. Rafe had an instant to note the startled dark brown eyes before the man cursed and stepped on the gas.

Against the rain-soaked pavement, the car's tires sent up a howling squeal as they fought for traction. Then they caught and the rear end fishtailed, slamming into Rafe's thigh. The blow knocked him into a sideways stumble and he hit the pavement hard, sprawling on the grit.

He'd barely dragged in a breath when the squeal of brakes jerked his chin up. The Crown Vic did a wild spinning U-turn. The driver gunned the engine. The car lurched forward.

Rafe scrambled to his feet. When the car rocketed for him, he dived for the curb.

"You're sure he said his name was Young?" Liz Scott asked, her voice foggy with sleep. "*Detective* Young?"

"Positive," Allie replied. "Liz, I'm sorry I woke you, but I've got a bad feeling about this. Why would a cop call and tell me my warehouse had been broken into if it hadn't been?"

"And the alarm panel says the system is still activated?"

"Yes, I—"

Allie jerked around when the roar of an engine and high squeal of rubber on pavement pierced the air. Instead of the police car she was hoping to see, she spotted a dark car whip a U-turn, then speed toward a man in the middle of the street.

"Look out!" she screamed even as the man dived out of the car's path.

"What the hell's going on?" Liz shouted.

"A car almost hit a man."

Allie screamed again when the car swerved, aiming right for him.

Her scalp prickled when the man's arm swung up and light glinted off the barrel of a gun aimed at the car's windshield. Two high-pitched pops exploded through the air.

The engine gave a deafening roar while the car veered wildly. Seconds later, it crashed head-on into the wall of a warehouse. Windows in the building shattered while metal screeched as it tore and bent.

Allie's stunned gaze jerked back to the man with the gun. Not any man, she realized when he stepped into a pool of light. *Rafe!*

"Oh, my God!"

"What? What the hell's going on?"

"It's Rafe!"

Allie didn't stop to think about her safety. Her single driving need was to get to Rafe.

She dropped her phone and tote and ran.

"Rafe!"

Gun gripped in both hands, he was halfway to the car when her shout had him turning toward her. Whatever he yelled back was lost against the roaring of her heart.

"Rafe!" She skidded to a stop inches from him. In the wan light, his mouth was a thin line, his eyes like hard black marbles.

"Are you okay?" she panted.

"Fine. Stay back while I check on the guy in the car."

Allie was suddenly aware that the air had turned heavy with the reek of gasoline.

A whoosh had her spinning toward the car just as flames danced from beneath its crumpled hood.

"I have to get the guy out of there," Rafe said, then headed toward the car.

Allie dashed to keep up with his long-legged stride.

He shot her a sideways look. "I said stay back. The car could explode at any second."

"Two can get him out faster than one." Closer now, she could see into the driver's window. "He's slumped over the steering wheel. He must be unconscious."

Rafe's hand clamped on her upper arm, staying her steps. "That's what it looks like." His voice was flat, his eyes remote. "Stay here while I check him."

"But—"

His hand tightened on her arm. "Dammit, he might be faking. He might have a gun."

Allie nodded numbly. Her stomach clenched while she watched Rafe advance to the driver's window, gun aimed at the motionless figure. He reached in, shook the guy's shoulder.

In the glare of the flames she saw the dark crimson stains on Rafe's fingers when he pulled back his hand. He stuck the gun in the back waistband of his jeans and jerked the car door open.

Allie dashed to the car as scarlet tongues of flames shot skyward. Black, acrid smoke rolled from beneath the crumpled hood, nearly obscuring her vision.

Rafe unhooked the seat belt, grabbed the unconscious man by the shoulders, then dragged him sideways.

"Grab his feet," Rafe shouted.

Allie gripped the man's ankles and lifted. Instantly, she staggered beneath his weight while her lungs fought to pull in scalding air that reeked of smoke and gasoline.

They'd barely made it halfway across the street when the fire's roar intensified.

A heartbeat later, an explosion blasted the air. A fist of heat and force fumed out, slamming her to the ground.

Chapter 6

Stunned by the blast, Allie gingerly sat up. Her ears rang. Her spine felt as if some giant hand had smashed into it, then flung her forward like a rag doll. Her palms stung from her crash-landing on the gritty pavement. Her right knee throbbed.

Glass crunched under Rafe's feet as he crouched beside her. "Are you okay?"

She looked up, trying to focus on his face through eyes stinging from the fire's acrid black smoke. "I…think so. You?"

"Fine." Gripping her arms, he helped her to her feet. "He's not," he said flatly, looking at the man lying in the street. "He's dead. Probably was before we pulled him out of the car."

Allie struggled to make out the man's features in the orange glare of the flames, which was hard to do because blood covered the entire right side of his head. His open eyes had the same dead stare she'd witnessed when she found Mercedes McKenzie.

The reminder tightened her stomach.

"Do you know him?" Rafe asked.

The question jerked her head around. "Shouldn't I be asking you that? You're the one he tried to run down."

Without comment, Rafe flipped open his cell phone and dialed 911.

While he spoke to the dispatcher, Allie shifted her gaze to the car. Sharp, brilliant tongues of flame had turned it into a blazing inferno. It had crashed head-on into a warehouse, shattering several windows and layering the street with shards of glass that glittered like a crimson sea in the fire's light.

Rafe closed his phone. "Police and fire are on the way."

Allie remembered the call she'd made. "Liz, too, probably."

"Liz?" Rafe asked as he slid his phone into a back pocket of his black jeans.

"My friend, Liz Scott. She's an OCPD sergeant. I was on the phone with her when I saw the car try to run you down." Suddenly aware of the stinging pain in her hands, Allie glanced at her palms and saw skinned flesh.

Rafe clamped a hand on her elbow. "Doesn't look like you're totally okay."

"They're just scrapes," she said as he steered her to a grassy spot on the edge of the street.

"Sit. I've got a first aid kit in my car."

"Fine. Can I borrow your phone? I dropped mine when all the excitement started. I need to call Liz and let her know we're safe."

After handing her his phone, Rafe jogged off.

With the odor of gas hanging thick and oily in the smoky air, Allie settled onto the curb. Careful of the nicks in her palm, she dialed her friend's number.

"Are you okay?" Liz shouted. "It sounded like all hell broke loose. I've been calling your cell for the past fifteen minutes. When you didn't answer, I pulled on some clothes and jumped in my car."

"I'm okay," Allie said, then briefed her friend on what had happened.

"Stay put. I'll be there in ten minutes."

"I'm not going anywhere," Allie said before ending the call.

With the shock from the explosion having cleared, a myriad of questions formed in her head. Who was the dead man lying in the street? Why had he tried to run Rafe down? And why the heck was Rafe even there?

Her gaze went to the main entrance to the warehouse facility. Where was Detective Young or the police officer he said would meet her? Why had Young called to tell her a burglar had kicked in the door to her warehouse and set off her alarm when it didn't appear either had happened?

She was still trying to come up with answers when Rafe reappeared, a metal first aid kit gripped in one hand. Two water bottles dangled from the other. Towering over her, dressed totally in black, with the fire leaping in the background, he looked lean and fit and a little on the dangerous side.

"Thanks for the phone," she said, handing it to him when he settled on the curb beside her. "Liz is on her way."

In the distance, a siren sounded. "We'll have a lot of company soon." He twisted the cap off one bottle and handed it to her.

Holding it by her fingertips, Allie took a sip. The tepid water felt like nirvana against her parched throat.

After taking a long swig from his own bottle, Rafe popped the lid on the first aid kit. "Hold out your hand."

"You're going to a lot of trouble for a couple of scrapes."

His expression grim, he tore open a packet containing an antiseptic wipe. "You wouldn't have those scrapes if you had stayed back like I told you to."

Allie winced when he swabbed her palm. "If I had, it might have taken you longer to get that guy as far from the car as we got him. Meaning, you'd have been closer to the explosion."

Rafe kept his head lowered while he positioned a bandage over the deepest scrape. "Maybe."

"Probably," she countered, still gritting her teeth against the sting of antiseptic.

He opened another packet and went to work on her other hand.

When he tilted her palm toward the illumination from one of the security lights, she had a close-up view of the strong, tanned column of his throat. Of the way his thick, black hair grazed the collar of the black T-shirt that clung to his chest and shoulders, revealing an awesome array of muscles. She was helpless to control the shiver that raced beneath her flesh.

Only moments ago she'd almost gotten blown to bits. Then there was the dead body lying a few feet away. The fact that she could get turned on in the midst of all that sent a gut-clenching uneasiness through her. Her mind skittered back to the hot, steamy dream she'd been trapped in when her phone rang. Even now she could picture Rafe positioned over her, their bodies linked while his hands glided across her sweat-slicked flesh.

Suddenly, the night seemed to press in on her, bringing to the surface a reminder of the vow she'd made long ago to draw an invisible line and never allow anyone to get so close that they mattered too much.

She had broken that vow with the friendship she'd formed with Liz and Claire. But her parents had taught her well and she wasn't prepared to cross that line with a man. Any man. Ever.

She tugged her hand free from Rafe's and shifted her thoughts to the here and now. "You asked me if I knew the dead man. Why?"

"Do you?"

"I've never seen him before. You're the one he tried to run down. Don't you know who he is?"

"No."

"Then why did he try to kill you?"

"I don't know." Rafe closed the lid on the first aid kit. "I also have no idea why he followed you here tonight."

She stared at him for a moment. "He *followed* me?"

"Yes. Did a good job of it, too. He varied the car's speed. Even let a pickup pull in front of him at one point."

"How do you know all that?"

"Because I tailed him from your house. He was parked on a side street that had a view of the only way in and out of that ritzy neighborhood you live in. When you turned onto the street, he flipped on his headlights and pulled in behind you."

Allie listened in dismay while her mind spun, trying to process the information. "First off, what were you doing outside of my house?"

"I had a gut feeling there might have been something to Ellen Bishop's threat." Rafe shrugged. "So I hung around after I followed you home from the auction."

"Do you think Ellen called this guy? That she sent him to hurt me?"

"If he wanted to hurt you, he had plenty of chance to do that on the drive here. He could have run you off the road. Shot you. Or rushed at you when you got to the door of your warehouse, then forced you to open it." Rafe took a long swallow of water. "His intent wasn't to hurt you. It was to watch you."

"Why?"

"Good question," Rafe said as the wail of sirens grew louder. "Why did you come here in the middle of the night?"

"A detective called me," she answered, then gave him the details of the conversation. She shifted her gaze to her car, parked in the pool of light in front of her warehouse. "When I got to the door, I saw that it hadn't been kicked in. And the alarm system's still activated."

Her hand trembling, she gestured toward the dead man. "He must have been the guy who called me."

"I'd say so. Too bad we don't know why."

"Your reasons for thinking he didn't intend to hurt me make sense," she said while her stomach clenched. "Even so, I'm thankful you were here. And that you're safe."

The urgent whipping sirens split the night as a dazzlingly lit fire truck turned into the entrance to the warehouse complex. Behind it sped a black and white police car, its light bar flashing red and blue. A sporty Miata brought up the rear.

"That's Liz's car," Allie said.

Rafe looked back at her, his expression unreadable. "Just so you'll know, the wreck didn't kill the guy," he said levelly. "I shot him."

* * *

By dawn, the warehouse complex was awash with portable lights, cops, the ME and their various vehicles. Yellow crime-scene tape blocked access to the area.

Arms crossed over his chest, Rafe leaned against a black and white patrol car, waiting. When the cops arrived, he and Allie had been separated for individual interviews. He'd given his statement to a uniformed officer, who told him a detective would speak with him shortly.

It was the same drill he'd gone through seven years ago when his life transformed into a nightmare. He'd been innocent of the crime he was accused of, but that hadn't mattered. Now he stood in the already skin-soaking early morning heat, having admitted to shooting the bastard driving the Crown Vic.

Rafe knew cops. To some, it wouldn't matter that he'd been exonerated and his conviction wiped off the books. With the Internet, nothing ever went away—all anyone had to do was run a search on his name and they'd get any number of hits on the newspaper articles from his trial.

He would forever be an ex-con, who spent two years locked up with the dregs of society—it was a short mental step to assume some of their evilness had rubbed off on him. As proof, early that morning he'd killed a man.

That knowledge dredged up memories and emotions—pain and fear swirling furiously inside him. The pain was an old companion. The fear was for the control he felt slipping, sliding through his grasp like smoke.

Movement across the parking lot at the door to Allie's warehouse caught his attention. Earlier she, her pal Liz Scott and a uniformed officer had gone to check the warehouse to determine if it actually had been broken into. Now Liz Scott emerged from the building.

Rafe watched the cop advance toward him with long, purposeful strides. She was dressed in a green blouse and black slacks, a gold badge and holstered automatic pistol clipped to the waistband. Her long red hair was held back in a braid that looped over one shoulder.

"Rafe, I'm Sergeant Scott," she said when she reached him. Up close, he saw the smattering of freckles across her nose and a cop's intensity in her pale green eyes. "Sounds like you had a busy evening."

"That's right."

"Tell me about it." She pulled a small notepad and pen from the pocket of her slacks. "From the beginning."

Pulling in a deep breath, he started with the threat that Ellen Bishop made against Allie during the silent auction.

Liz jotted notes as he went through the events that followed, asking a question here and there.

He ended his statement, saying, "After I dived out of its path, the Crown Vic swerved toward me. I fired my weapon twice. I didn't see that I had a choice."

Liz closed the flap on her notepad. "I imagine it will ease your mind to know that Allie has made it clear the driver tried to run you down. I'll review the statement you gave to the patrol officer. If I have questions after I get reports from the lab and the ME, I'll contact you."

"You're working this case?"

She nodded. "My permanent assignment is to the cold-case office, but I used to work out of Homicide. After Allie called and told me about the dead guy here, I phoned my captain, told him I didn't have anything urgent on my plate and volunteered to work this case. He said yes."

"Being Allie's friend, I expect you know my history."

"You bet I do," she said, eyeing him. "You're wondering if I'm one of those police officers who can't admit the system makes mistakes."

"I've run into a few cops like that."

"Yeah, well, I'm not one of them. You've got a rep of being a damn good PI with a legal permit to carry a concealed weapon." She angled her chin. "It wasn't too shabby the way you dealt with that money-laundering street gang a few years back. The lieutenant over at the department's Gang Squad gives you full credit for obtaining the evidence that sent the entire gang leadership to prison."

Rafe frowned. "Did you have time to find all that out tonight?"

"I checked you out a few days ago when Allie told me you'd shown up at Silk & Secrets."

"Why bother? I went there on behalf of my client, to ask questions about her finding the McKenzie woman's body."

"So you claimed. But you and Allie share an uncomfortable past and that isn't something I was willing to ignore. She's a good friend of mine. I wanted to make sure you hadn't been carrying around a chip on your shoulder and all of a sudden decided a little revenge was in order against a woman who helped send you to prison."

"Did I pass your test?" Rafe was aware of the cold hardness that had settled in his voice. If the cop took exception to his tone, she didn't show it.

"With flying colors. Now that we've got the past out of the way, let's talk about our dead guy here." As she spoke, Liz's gaze drifted past Rafe to where the ME's assistant was crouched beside the body. "Name's Joseph Slater. That ring any bells?"

"No."

Liz's gaze swung back to meet Rafe's. "I think your theory that he had plenty of chances to hurt Allie if that had been his intent is right on. What does your gut tell you, Diaz? Do you really think Ellen Bishop sent Slater? That what happened tonight is connected to Mercedes McKenzie's murder?"

Rafe scrubbed a hand over his jaw. Knowing he wasn't minutes away from getting hauled to jail for murder had something loosening inside him. "I don't know. But it's worth looking into."

Liz arched an auburn brow. "Are you going to be looking into it?"

Rafe matched her steady stare. "Even if I wasn't trying to clear a client accused of murdering McKenzie, I'd check it out. Call me curious, but anytime someone tries to run me down, I want to know why."

"Same here. When I have a chance, I'll get with the detectives working the McKenzie homicide and take a look at the file." Liz handed him a business card. "I'll get your phone number off the uniform's report. How about you and I keep in touch if we find a connection between the cases?"

"Deal." As Rafe slid the card into his back pocket, he caught movement in his peripheral vision. Turning his head, he spotted Allie coming across the parking lot, her tote bag slapping against her side as she hurried their way.

In a red sleeveless top smudged from pavement grit and jeans ripped at the right knee, she looked deceptively delicate. But Rafe knew it hadn't been some shrinking violet who, with no thought to her own safety, helped him drag Slater away from the burning car.

For the first time, Rafe acknowledged that the details he'd

begun collecting on the woman she had become didn't at all match the spoiled, self-involved rich girl he'd vaguely known.

"You won't believe this," Allie said when she reached them. Up close, he saw that her blue eyes were tense and grim, her mouth clamped in a thin line.

"What's wrong, Al?" Liz asked.

"Claire's husband just called. He was on his way to the Reunion Square bakery when he glanced in the window of my shop. It's been burglarized."

Feeling cold, numb and faintly sick, Allie stood in the center of her shop. Silk robes and gowns that had once hung on padded hangers were pooled on the floor in an ocean of vivid, sensual color. Drawers had been emptied of satin bustiers, lacy bras and panties, the items flung here and there, tornado-style. Display cases stood open, their contents scattered across the polished wood floor to form a sparkling path of glittering hair accessories, jeweled purses and sequined slippers.

"Jackson and I feel awful about this." Claire Castle squeezed Allie's hand. "I can't believe we live right next door and didn't hear a thing."

"Your apartment is upstairs over your shop." Allie felt a tug at her heart over the guilt in her friend's eyes. "It's not like the burglar came in here and smashed things. Tossing around lingerie and accessories doesn't exactly make a lot of noise."

"You're right." Sighing, Claire reached back to tug the band ponytailing her dark, glossy hair a little higher. "If only the alarm had gone off, we'd have heard it."

"There wasn't a chance of the thing going off." Rafe's deep voice coming from the rear of the showroom had both women turning toward the arched doorway that led to the shop's design area and fitting rooms.

It hit Allie that the man dressed all in black seemed to block out everything around him with his height and broad shoulders. The day-old stubble that now shadowed his jaw only made him look that much more compelling. Delectable.

Lord, here she was, standing in the chaos left by a burglar while lusting after a man. Too late, she rethought the wisdom of having agreed to Liz's suggestion that Rafe follow her to the shop while Liz finished tying up loose ends at the warehouse complex. But with the events of the night having left Allie feeling vulnerable, she had been grateful for the escort.

Had it only been the previous night when she and Rafe stood in the hotel's parking lot and she suggested they someday might become cautious friends? So much for caution, she thought. She couldn't even look at Rafe without feeling her blood heat and her pulse rate jolt.

"Why wasn't there a chance the alarm would go off?"

Claire's question jerked Allie back to the present. "I'm wondering the same thing. The alarm salesman assured me I purchased a quality product."

"Your high-dollar alarm would probably keep out most B&E guys," Rafe said. "But whoever broke in here knew what he was doing. After prying off the cover of the alarm panel mounted over the back entry door, he cut some existing wires and clipped new ones to bypass the old. It takes skill and a good understanding of how alarms work to pull that off."

"Great," Allie said. "I get hit by an intelligent burglar. How much better can this get?"

"It's about to get way better." Claire plucked a padded hanger off the floor. "Because I'm going to get started putting everything back in its place. As soon as Jackson gets off his conference call, he's coming over to pitch in, too."

Allie gave her friend a hug. "You don't know how much I appreciate that."

Claire arched a dark brow. "This coming from the woman who spent an entire week helping me clean ash and soot off my stock of antiques."

Even now, thinking about how Claire and Jackson had almost died in the fire at her antique shop set by an out-for-revenge former colleague of Jackson's had Allie's stomach clenching. They, along with Liz, were closer to Allie than any blood relative of hers had ever been.

"Do you know yet if anything's missing?" Rafe asked.

Allie shook her head. "I don't have a clue. With everything scattered around, it's impossible to tell."

"What about from your office?" He angled his chin toward the back room. "Should be easy to figure out if equipment is missing."

"Go take a look," Claire urged while sliding the straps of a frothy pink lace teddy onto the hanger. "Heaven knows I've pined after so many of these gorgeous creations that I don't have to ask which rack anything belongs on."

"Thanks," Allie said. "As soon as I take a look in the office, I'll be back out here to help."

"Shoo," Claire said, flicking a wrist her way.

When Allie stepped into her office, she groaned. The desk she kept pristine was now scattered with the files that had been organized in four separate drawers. Several folders lay open, their top pages covered with a gray fingerprint powder left by the crime-scene techs Liz had sent to the shop.

Allie swept her gaze around the small room. "My

computer's here. The fax. Shredder." She glanced inside the gaping door to the supply room. Bottles of cleaning products and stacks of office supplies had been swept off the shelves and now lay heaped on the floor. Crouching, she input her digital code into the panel on the small safe, then opened its door. "The petty cash is all here."

Rafe stood at the desk, gazing down at the sea of paper. "This file folder that's open on top has a printout of inventory in it. Are the items listed on it here in the shop?"

Allie walked to his side and picked up the printout. "No." She flipped through the pages. "This is for equipment at my warehouse. Office machines, the sewing machines my seamstresses use. New computer hardware we'll use next month when we start accepting orders through my Web site. There's also a listing of all the stock, the lingerie and accessories that are stored there. And the trousseaus I'm designing for three brides-to-be."

Rafe shuffled through the remainder of papers in the folder. "Everything in here lists a PO box for the warehouse."

"The only physical street address I use on correspondence is for this shop. I don't want my customers to get confused. If they had both addresses, they might go to the warehouse instead of coming here."

"If I wanted to know the actual street address of your warehouse, I'd go online to the county assessor's Web site to search yours and your company's name. Would either search bring up the address?"

"No. The warehouse is owned by a company under the Fielding family umbrella. It's that way for tax purposes."

Crossing his arms, Rafe leaned against the edge of the desk. "Let's go with the assumption that the now-deceased Joseph Slater burglarized this place. He was after a specific item, but didn't find it. So, he trashes your desk and discovers the file on your warehouse. In it, he sees the list of inventory. Bingo, the item he's after is listed. But that only gets him so far because all he's got on the warehouse is a PO box. How's he going to get the actual address at three o'clock in the morning?"

Allie shoved a hand through her hair. "By calling me, pretending to be a detective and saying that the warehouse had been broken into. And that I needed to meet him there."

Rafe nodded. "Your home address is listed in the phone book, so all he had to do was wait until you headed for the warehouse and follow you. You parked right at the front door."

"I wish to hell I knew what Slater was after."

"That, and who sent him, are the million-dollar questions."

Allie felt a sudden chill. "When Slater saw which warehouse was mine, I wonder if he had time to call someone and tell them where it is? Someone who might try to break in."

Rafe nodded, his eyes grim. "That's a possibility. After we're done here, let's go back there."

"And look for what?"

"Something out of place, maybe. Or a package brought in by an employee that doesn't belong there. Could be anything."

He pushed away from the desk, grabbed the phone book that had been tossed on the floor and fanned through it. "I'll give you the name and number of a security company I've worked with." He unearthed a notepad and pen from the desktop clutter and jotted the information. "Until it's clear what's going on, it'd be a good idea to hire them to watch the warehouse and the shop while no one's there."

"I'll arrange for them to start today." She jabbed the paper he handed her into the back pocket of her jeans, then stared down at the inventory list. "Dammit, if I knew what they wanted, I'd give it to them."

"Just like that?" Rafe asked.

"Just like that." Too on-edge to keep still, she paced to the other side of the office. At the door she turned and moved back the other way. "Everything in this shop, in the warehouse, can be replaced. It's simply a matter of money."

"To most people, that's a big deal."

The bluntness in his tone had Allie halting midstep. She turned and faced him. "But not to the heiress of the Fielding fortune, you mean," she said levelly.

"As I recall, you used to go through money like it was water. Men, too."

"True enough. I had my own reasons for behaving the way I did in college. Then circumstances changed. I did, too. But it's clear you don't want to acknowledge that." She could hear her emotions unraveling in her voice, but there wasn't anything she could do about it. "The bottom line is, whatever it is I have that someone else wants, it's not worth losing a life over. Which is what almost happened to you this morning. So whatever its value, I would give it to them." She snapped her fingers. "Just like that."

She turned away, intending to join Claire in the showroom. She'd made it as far as the door when Rafe gripped her arm, spun her around and pressed her back against the wall.

He stared down at her, his dark eyes intense. "Who the hell are you?"

"Why ask when you seem to have me all figured out?" she flung back. Just the feel of his hands on her bare arms turned her insides to molten glass.

"I thought I did. Shallow. Spoiled. A party girl used to having men fall at her feet." He took her hair in his hand. "There are layers now. Contrasts."

Her heart dropped to her toes, then bounced up again. The dream she'd had of them together paled in the reality of his body brushing against hers. Of the soft caress of his warm breath on her cheek.

His fingers combed through her hair. "You design expensive lingerie and sell it to your rich friends. Then you dress in old clothes and go off to paint houses for abused women."

"So?" The electricity in the air was getting thick enough to drink. Allie could literally taste it on her tongue.

"So last night at the hotel, I overheard you arranging to donate personal funds to the foundation that match the total the silent auction brought in."

"It's rude to eavesdrop." She tried for a casual tone but only succeeded in sounding breathless.

"Sue me," he murmured. "At the warehouse, you didn't give a thought to your own safety when you insisted on helping me drag Slater out of that burning car."

"Anyone would have done that."

"Funny, I can't picture drunken Ellen Bishop putting herself in harm's way to help someone." Very slowly, very deliberately, his hand came up to cup her cheek.

Allie watched his eyes darken. Saw his gaze drop to her mouth. So she couldn't pretend later, even to herself, that she didn't see the kiss coming.

She tried to think, to remember the consequences if she allowed him to cross that invisible line she'd drawn long ago. But her senses had clouded and all she could do was feel.

"I'm…not sure this is a good idea, considering," she managed.

"You're probably right, considering." He ran the pad of his thumb over her bottom lip. "But I can't think of a better one right now," he added, then captured her mouth with his.

Chapter 7

Rafe Diaz kissed like a fallen angel, coaxing and enticing and unrelenting. He didn't let up; didn't allow Allie to breathe. He just kissed her, slow and sure and endlessly, until she began to feel faint from the uneasy, exhilarating awareness that no man had ever kissed her this way.

There was nothing soft about him; not the magnificent shoulders her fingers clenched, not his hands that cupped her face, not his lips or tongue. Nothing.

She wanted, as she had never wanted before. Never dreamed of wanting. The ache was so huge it left no room for reason. The rightness of it was so clear that it left no room for doubt. There was only this moment. This man.

A whimpering moan rose in the back of her throat. It wasn't due to protest or pain, but of no-holds-barred desire.

For Rafe, the sound that seemed to claw up from her throat was every bit as primitive as the need that raged through him. He'd known desire before, but not this gnawing, tearing desperation.

His hands slid from her face, across her shoulders, down her trim, toned body to grip her hips. When she strained against him, center to center, core to core, he was ready to rip off her jeans and feed those hungers. More than willing to take what he craved without a thought for the consequences.

Consequences.

He slapped his palms on the wall on either side of her head to stop himself from touching. From taking. Fighting to regain both his breath and his control, he eased out of the kiss. Stepped back.

What the *hell* was he doing?

He knew better than anyone that every act carried consequences. He'd walked out of prison and painstakingly rebuilt a life centered around ironclad restraint. It was clear now that this gorgeous, intriguing woman had the power to whisk away every bit of his control as if it were nothing but dust in the wind.

He'd be damned if he let her. Damned if he'd allow himself to be ruled by emotion.

Curling his hands into fists, he studied her while she leaned back against the wall, her blond hair tousled, her eyes closed, the lips that had taken him so close to the edge of reason slightly parted. By the time her lashes fluttered up and her blue eyes focused on his, he had his control snapped back ruthlessly in place.

"You were right," he said. "That wasn't a good idea."

Allie might have flinched from the remark if she hadn't been braced against the wall. Everything inside her was in a mindless rush—her heart, her blood, her brain—and the man responsible now claimed that kissing her had been a bad idea. Maybe when her senses cleared and reason returned she would agree, but how the hell could he sound so contained and unaffected when the same kiss had pummeled her insides into nuclear meltdown?

She searched the hard planes of his face, trying to find some hint of emotion, a flicker of feeling, but there was none.

Her pride scratched, she forced her mouth to curve. "It's good we're in agreement," she said, infusing her voice with a coolness that contrasted with the fire blazing in her system.

Just then, his cell phone rang. Rafe dug it out of his pocket, checked the display. "I have to take this."

"Of course."

On legs that felt like molten glass, Allie stepped to her cluttered desk. Looking down, she stared unseeingly at the sea of papers and file folders covered with a fine dusting of fingerprint powder. It was true that no man had ever driven her to almost complete abandon with just a kiss, but there was something more. Something…

She went very still as emotion delivered a punch to her heart. Shaken, she turned and looked at Rafe. Phone pressed to his ear, he stood with his back to her, all tall and tough-bodied, his deep voice a quiet murmur on the air. For an instant, she was back in his arms, his mouth plundering hers while a closeness that felt utterly foreign from anything she'd experienced with another man swept through her.

She closed her eyes while the wariness with which she lived every day of her life had her breath going shallow. She had no idea what alien emotion had caused that finger-snap connection to Rafe nor did she want to find out. At this point, all she wanted was the safety of distance.

He ended the call, flipped his phone closed and turned.

His face was tense, his eyes cheerless in the office's bright light. "I know I said I'd go to your warehouse with you, but first I've got to meet Hank Bishop."

"I know how it is when a client calls. You have to go," Allie flicked a wrist toward the office's door. "I'll ask Claire to go with me. Maybe Liz can meet us. They've both been there before so they might help spot something out of place." And because the unexpected, unwanted emotions still battered her, Allie added, "You're definitely not needed."

"Even so, I want to see what you've got inside."

"It's mainly three floors of lingerie, sewing areas and offices."

He walked back toward her, his gaze locked on hers. "Slater needed to know the location of your warehouse because there's something inside he wanted. Or he at least thought it was there. He's dead, but if he was working for someone, that person is still after whatever it is." Rafe checked his watch. "How about I meet you and your friends there in about an hour and a half?"

Allie swept her gaze around her ravaged office. He was right. She'd been lured to her warehouse by a man who had tried to kill Rafe. If he could help figure out what Slater was after—and who sent him—they could all get back to their own lives that much sooner.

"Fine," she said, using the same, void-of-emotion tone she heard in his voice. "See you there."

In the meantime, because the lust crawling around in her belly seemed to be all one-sided, she would do her damnedest to just get over it.

Rafe stepped onto a freight elevator in a vacant downtown building, jerked the wooden door down and stabbed the button for the top floor. With half its windows boarded up and the other half shut tight, the building was one huge oven.

After a plaintive groan from its motor, the elevator began to rise with a combination of hair-raising metallic squeals and a pronounced shimmy.

He set his jaw. Maybe the damn thing would lock up. Maybe he'd get stuck there and bake to death. If so, he'd have something to think about other than Allie. The feel of her body's subtle curves and long lines beneath his hands. Her erotic scent that still clouded his lungs. The flicker of withdrawal he'd seen in her eyes when she agreed the kiss had been a bad idea.

"Damn," he muttered. "Damn. Damn."

He ought to be glad he'd gotten out of that shop where the very air carried her scent. Happy that he had time to get his system leveled before he saw her again.

And when he did, he needed to focus on his case.

That was, after all, the kind of life he had chosen to live when he walked out of prison, solitary with only business matters to deal with. He didn't want to be touched emotionally. Didn't want to open himself to the trouble he knew all too well personal involvement of any kind could bring.

Even so, he wasn't going to kid himself. It was apparent the grand plan he'd made for his life seemed to pale whenever he got around Allie. Bottom line, he was going to have to be more machine than man in order to keep a grip on control.

The elevator shuddered to a halt. Rafe shoved the door up and stepped into a vast area where all interior walls had been gutted. With only concrete pillars still standing, he had a clear view of Hank Bishop and his partner and brother-in-law, Guy Jones, at the far side of the building near an open window. Another man—tall, lanky and nearly bald—was with them.

When Hank Bishop looked up, he excused himself from the others and headed Rafe's way.

Dressed in a green golf shirt, tan slacks and loafers without socks, Bishop's footsteps echoed off the concrete floor. In the time since Rafe had last seen his client, Bishop seemed to have aged ten years. The lines at the corners of his eyes and mouth had deepened, the gray at his temples was more pronounced.

Understandable, with a murder charge hanging over the real estate developer's head, Rafe thought.

"Thanks for meeting me here instead of my office," Bishop said as Rafe returned his handshake. "Guy forgot to tell me until the last minute that he'd made an appointment for us with the Realtor who's trying to dump this monstrosity on an unsuspecting buyer."

Rafe swept his gaze over the vacant expanse. "What did this building used to be?"

"A department store. Guy thinks renovating it into lofts and apartments will be a for-sure moneymaker."

"You don't agree?" Rafe knew this area of downtown was undergoing a massive revitalization. Numerous old buildings had already been converted for housing and retail use.

"It would make a super investment if the foundation wasn't cracked. And the walls weren't insulated with asbestos. Then there's the mold that's turned the basement fuzzy. Fixing all that will add a couple of mil to the renovation costs."

Bishop's gaze focused on the two men who were now

deep in conversation. "Since the day he married my baby sister and we became partners, I've been telling Guy we're in a business that requires thinking outside the box. He's still trying to grasp that concept."

With a restless move of his shoulders, Bishop looked back at Rafe. "I don't expect you're here to talk real estate."

"No, we need to discuss a couple of things that happened last night."

Bishop's expression turned somber. "Guy told me about Ellen getting drunk at the auction and confronting Allie Fielding. It's hard to believe Ellen did that."

"It wasn't pretty."

Bishop ran a hand down the back of his neck. "Looking back, I was a fool to hook up with Mercedes. All I managed to do was hurt my family. And get arrested for a murder I didn't commit."

"The only way to get you clear of that is to find out who the real killer is. Meaning, you need to level with me."

Bishop looked vaguely surprised. "I have."

"You told me there was no way your wife could have found out about your affair with Mercedes before she was murdered."

"I don't know that Ellen did find out."

"You don't know she didn't. Last night, she had a few drinks too many and got verbally and physically abusive just because a shopkeeper did business with both her and your mistress. Your wife doesn't strike me as a woman who'd hold back if she found out you'd moved your mistress into a condo and were paying all her bills. That's a hell of a lot more than a casual affair. Any wife would view that as insulting and threatening, and maybe do something about it."

"Dammit, I know Ellen. She would have confronted me, not Mercedes."

"You *think* you know your wife, but she surprised you by getting in Allie Fielding's face last night," Rafe countered. "I need to know if there's anyone who knew about your affair, who might have told Ellen." Rafe glanced at Guy Jones, deep in conversation with the Realtor. "What about your brother-in-law? He might have mentioned the affair to his wife."

"No. I purposely kept Guy in the dark about Mercedes for that very reason. I didn't want anyone in the family to know." Bishop looked away, his hands curving into fists. "There's one person who might have told Ellen."

"Who?"

"Matt Weber. He was my personal pilot for years. I fired him over a month ago because he showed up at the airport smelling of booze an hour before he was scheduled to fly me to a business conference. He asked me to give him a second chance and got ticked when I said no."

"You're sure he knew about you and Mercedes?"

"He'd flown us on trips a couple of times. He also flew Ellen to New York when she wanted to shop. After I fired him, I reported Weber's drinking to the FAA, which is the kiss of death in this country for a pilot. To get back at me, he could have tipped Ellen off about Mercedes."

"Do you know where Weber is now?"

"I heard he got a job flying freight from Singapore to Taipei. I have no idea who hired him."

"I'll try to track him down," Rafe said, committing the pilot's name to memory.

"You said you need to discuss a couple of things about last night. What else?"

For no other reason than he'd had shots in the dark score direct hits before, Rafe asked, "Does the name Joseph Slater ring a bell?"

"Joe Slater?" Bishop's forehead furrowed in puzzlement. "Don't tell me he showed up at the silent auction."

"So you know him?"

"I know *of* him. He used to be a builder. Got into trouble with the locals over code violations and with the Feds over taxes. After his company went down the tubes, Slater let people in the business know his services were for hire."

"What sort of services?"

"Undercutting competitors."

"How?"

Bishop slid a hand into the pocket of his khakis. "Suppose Company A decides to bid on a project but wants to know what its top competitor, Company B, is planning to bid. Company A hires Slater to get the information. Company A submits the lowest bid and wins the contract."

"How would Slater go about getting the information?"

"Company A doesn't care and doesn't want to know. My guess is it would involve some breaking and entering or computer hacking to get a look at Company B's files."

"That sounds like a big risk."

Bishop lifted a shoulder. "Might be one worth taking if a multimillion dollar contract is up for grabs."

"Did you ever hire Slater?"

"Hell no. My personal life might be in shambles, but I go by the rules when it comes to business."

Rafe thought about the burglary at Silk & Secrets. "Would Slater know his way around an alarm system?"

"He'd have had one installed in every place he built. He

could have watched the alarm people, asked questions and learned. Why are you asking about Slater?"

"I suspect he disabled the alarm at Allie Fielding's shop last night and burglarized it. When he didn't find what he was looking for, he called her, pretending to be a cop and told her someone had broken into her warehouse. When she left to meet him, he followed her there."

Bishop frowned. "Mercedes sold a line of purses out of Allie's shop. They're manufactured at Allie's warehouse. Are you thinking Slater had something to do with Mercedes's murder?"

"It's possible. All I know for sure is that Slater wanted inside the warehouse. That might just be a huge coincidence, but I'm not willing to overlook it. Especially since he tried to run me down."

Bishop looked stunned. "Slater tried to kill you?"

Rafe nodded. "He's the one who wound up dead. The fact you knew of him means anyone connected with you— your wife, your son who works for you, your business partner—all might have heard of him, too. And hired him to kill Mercedes."

"Why?"

"I don't know. But think about this. Your mistress had recording equipment installed in every room of the condo. The only reason she would do that is to record conversations. Maybe she did that to sell information. Or blackmail someone."

Bishop scrubbed at his forehead with his fingertips. "Has anyone thought that Mercedes could have been a victim of a random crime? That she just walked in on some burglar and died because she was in the wrong place at the wrong time?"

"If that was the case, property most likely would have

been missing from the scene. At the very least, the bracelet she was wearing when her body was found would have been long gone." Rafe narrowed his eyes. "Did you notice it when you got to the condo and found her body?"

"I was focused on the fact that she was dead," Bishop shot back. "What bracelet are you talking about?"

"The twin to the one your wife had on last night. The diamonds are heart-shaped. Apparently, you bought a matching one for Mercedes."

"That's right. She saw a picture of Ellen wearing her bracelet. Mercedes pouted about wanting one like it, so I had it made. But she couldn't have been wearing it the night she died."

"Why?"

"The clasp came loose so I took it to a jeweler for repair before the murder. With all that's gone on, I forgot about it until right now." Bishop dug his billfold out of his back pocket. "I've got the jeweler's claim ticket. The bracelet is still there."

"Maybe Mercedes checked to see if the repair work was finished? It was, so she picked it up herself."

"She didn't know what jeweler I took the bracelet to." Bishop scowled at the claim ticket. "If this wasn't Sunday, I'd call right now and find out if they still have it."

"Why don't you let me check with the jeweler in the morning?" Already it sounded like there was something strange going on with the bracelet. If that was the case, Rafe wanted to find out for himself.

The hard clip of footsteps had him looking up in time to see Guy Jones headed their way.

"Diaz, you look like you had a rough night," he said, pausing beside Rafe.

"You might say that," he said, scrubbing a hand over his stubbled jaw. His watching Allie's boathouse had turned into a hell of a lot more than a simple stakeout.

"I'm in the same boat. My wife and I spent a couple of hours after we left the auction trying to get Ellen sober."

Jones turned his attention to his brother-in-law. "The Realtor's got another party interested in this building. This location is prime. I say we make an offer and put down a deposit before it slips away."

Bishop crossed his arms over his chest. "It'll take millions just to bring this place up to code. You want to make a personal investment in it, fine. The company isn't touching it."

Rafe watched Jones's brows knit in a single dark line of temper. "Dammit, this neighborhood is on the rise. Every piece of property in it is positioned to triple in value."

"Then you ought to have no problem using your own money to buy the place."

"My own money is mostly tied up right now in paying for the dream wedding Katie's always wanted."

"Sorry, Guy. This place just isn't a sound investment."

"Forget it." Jones sliced a hand through the air. "But you're making a mistake that's gonna cost our company big." With that, he turned and stalked off.

"I'll catch hell from my baby sister for upsetting him," Bishop muttered. "Want some advice, Diaz? Don't go into business with a relative."

"I'll keep that in mind."

"Look, let's get back to the bracelet. I bought Mercedes a half-dozen gold ones, all with different types of gems. It's possible Allie's wrong about which one Mercedes had on. After all, Allie had just found her dead. She was probably in shock. Maybe you should recheck that with her. Make sure."

"I plan to." Accepting fate, Rafe slid the claim check into the pocket. Even if he wanted to avoid Allie, it'd be damn hard to do the way her name kept cropping up in his investigation.

"It's too bad Liz got caught up in paperwork and couldn't meet us here," Claire Castle said after she and Allie finished checking all three floors of the warehouse. "Maybe she would have spotted something out of place."

Hands planted on her hips, Allie swept her gaze around the large, airy room where a dozen sewing machines sat at individual workstations. Cutting tables were positioned at the rear of the room. Shelves holding countless spools of thread in every color of the rainbow lined one entire wall.

Bolts of silk, satin, lace and ribbon were aligned according to color. Clear plastic containers held an array of the beads, spangles and pearls that would be handstitched onto purses and slippers.

As always, the floor was spotless, the shelves orderly, the workstations pristine.

"I doubt Liz would have had any more luck than we did," Allie said. "There just isn't anything out of place."

"You ought to know." Claire glanced around. "Do you still want to take the trousseau items to the shop?"

Allie shoved a hand through her hair and eased out a breath. She'd taken time to shower after she and Claire got the shop back into a halfway orderly state, but the hot water had done nothing to ease the throb in her right knee from her crash landing when Slater's car exploded. Or lessen the fatigue that made her eyes feel like they'd been scrubbed with sand. Then there was the whammy Rafe's kiss had delivered to her system. That she'd forgotten about the trousseau items was a clear sign her brain wasn't operating on all cylinders.

"Yes, thanks for the reminder," Allie said. "All three brides have appointments for fittings next week at the shop."

"It's not like you don't have plenty to deal with," Claire said, following Allie to a large closet. "You've been through enough to put anyone's emotions into overdrive."

Allie unhooked a hot pink garment bag off the closet's rod and handed it to Claire. "I did have an eventful night."

"Not to mention an interesting close encounter a couple of hours ago," Claire murmured as Allie carried two additional garment bags out of the closet.

Because Claire's husband had shown up to help straighten up the shop right after Rafe left, and the friends had driven separately to the warehouse, Allie had waited until they arrived to tell Claire about the kiss she and Rafe had shared. Although hours had passed, her insides still felt like scorched earth.

"*Interesting* isn't the word I'd use," Allie said as they laid the garment bags on one of the worktables. "Rafe and I agreed that kissing each other was a bad idea. In my opinion, that's true for several reasons."

"I take it one is what happened between you in the past."

Allie nodded. "I'm sure when he looks at me, he pictures me in that courtroom, testifying against him."

"You told the truth."

"Even so, he was innocent and went to prison partly because of my testimony. That's what you call heavy baggage."

"Okay, that's one reason," Claire said. "You said there were several."

"I'm not interested in getting involved in a serious relationship with any man. You know that."

"Yes, I do. And I understand why you feel that way. But you're being unfair to yourself to let the way your parents dealt with their own unhappiness rule how you live your life."

"It might be unfair, but that's the way it is." It still hurt. No matter how often Allie told herself it was foolish to dwell on what had happened so many years ago, the pain and confusion she suffered as a child still bled into the woman.

Claire leaned against the table. "Besides, just because you kiss a man who happens to be a mega-gorgeous hunk doesn't mean what's between you is destined to be serious. Why not spend some time together? Simply enjoy each other?"

Allie thought about the closeness she had experienced with Rafe that she'd felt with no other man. She hadn't mentioned that aftereffect of the kiss to Claire. No way could she begin to try to explain such an alien emotion when just the thought of it formed a ball of ice in her belly.

"Look, there's no chance two people can develop any kind of relationship when they don't see each other."

"Are you forgetting that Rafe called fifteen minutes ago to say he's on his way here?"

"I haven't forgotten. He's coming here on business. After I walk him through this place, I doubt our paths will cross again unless something about his investigation comes up. Heaven knows he has his hands full trying to get his client off the hook for Mercedes's murder. As for me, with the shop, my designs, the upcoming kickoff of my Web site and the foundation, I don't have a lot of spare time in my schedule."

"You could bring Rafe to dinner," Clair suggested. "It's our Sunday supper night and there's always plenty of food."

Allie gave her friend a narrow-eyed look. After Claire

and Jackson married, they had started the ritual of having Liz and Allie over for dinner one Sunday night each month. Sam Broussard had joined the group after he and Liz started dating. Claire, a consummate romantic, was forever urging Allie to bring a date. Allie never had. She doubted she would ever meet a man who mattered enough to share with her friends.

"Thanks, but inviting Rafe would be as bad an idea as our kissing was." Allie turned to the worktable. "I need to make sure all trousseau items are in each bag before I take them to my car."

"I have to make potato salad for tonight. Unless you need me to hang around, I'll take off."

"Go ahead." Allie gave her friend's arm a squeeze. "I appreciate all you and Jackson have done today. And on top of everything else, you're feeding me dinner."

Claire grinned. "That's what friends are for."

Ten minutes later, Allie had double checked the items inside two of the garment bags and was unzipping the third when she heard footsteps coming along the hallway.

Her fingers tightened reflexively on the zipper. She'd called the security guard now posted at the warehouse's front door and told him to let Rafe in when he arrived, so she knew who the footsteps belonged to.

Knew, too, it was ridiculous that just the prospect of seeing Rafe again had her pulse thudding hard and thick at the base of her throat. Nothing could develop between them.

She didn't *want* anything to develop.

Not with Rafe or any other man. She'd grown up watching people leave. Her mother. The seemingly endless succession of women her father married, then divorced. Even the servants she'd grown close to eventually moved on.

All that leaving had soured Allie on relationships in general.

Then she looked toward the doorway and saw Rafe. Tall, lean, his black hair mussed, looking impossibly masculine and sexy and in need of a shave. And that mouth, so beautifully sculpted, even if it did tend to scowl.

As her heartbeat slowed and thickened and the pounding of her pulse grew to mask all lesser sounds, she knew one thing she did want.

To feel that mouth on hers again.

Chapter 8

Rafe caught a whiff of Allie's alluring scent as he followed the security guard's directions along the warehouse's second-floor hallway. By the time he stepped through the door to the workroom and saw her, every muscle in his body was tight.

She stood before a long worktable, which held several hot pink garment bags. One of the bags was open, displaying a rainbow of pastel-colored silks.

Sometime after he'd left her shop, she had changed out of the red top and torn-at-the-knee jeans. Now she wore a sleeveless turquoise shell, black capris and black strappy sandals. Her hair was brushed back from her face in a long, waving stream of golden blond. Her lightly tanned skin looked spa-perfect.

When she looked up and met his gaze, the rush of emotion that sparked in her blue eyes was too scattered for him to interpret. Was she thinking about the kiss that had knocked him for a loop? Regretting it had happened? Wishing she'd pushed him away? Was she wondering—like he was—if she'd ever get his taste out of her system?

Just seeing her again had him wanting to drag her against him, capture her mouth with his all over again and plunder.

Not going to happen, he reminded himself. The insidious need that now sizzled to life inside of him every time he got around her could be controlled. *Had* to be controlled.

He blocked out the thought that there were some things between heaven and earth that weren't meant to be held in check. He was here on business. He'd take care of it, then get the hell away from this woman who with one look could shake the restraint he had believed so unshakable.

As he walked toward her, his gaze did a quick sweep of the room. It was spacious, filled with worktables, sewing machines and shelves that held bolts of frothy-colored fabric, ribbon and lace. He glanced into an open closet before pausing beside the table where Allie stood.

Up close, he saw that her cheeks were pale with fatigue. "I don't know about you," he began, "but this is turning out to be one heck of a long day."

When she nodded, light glittered as it caught the dangle of the dark blue stones at her ears. Their color was a shade darker than her eyes. "Claire and I were talking about everything that's happened since last night," she said. "Add 'little sleep' to the mix, and it's hard to take it all in."

"Speaking of Claire, I thought she and Liz would be here."

"Claire was. She had to leave to get some things done. Liz never made it. When I called to ask if she could meet us, she said she'd gotten held up at the station with paperwork."

"Too bad. I want to check if she's got any leads on who

hired Slater, which might point to why he wanted in here." Rafe checked his watch. "I'll try to get in touch with Liz later."

For an instant, a look of indecision settled in Allie's eyes.

"What?" he asked.

"Nothing." She reached into the unzipped garment bag and plucked out a beaded evening purse that looked like an oversized clamshell. "I just…had a thought about something." She laid the purse aside. "Did you learn anything from Hank Bishop?"

The speed at which she changed the subject had Rafe curious about what that something was.

"Maybe," he replied vaguely.

"I shouldn't have asked." As she spoke, Allie removed several padded hangers from the garment bag that held what looked like an assortment of robes, gowns and other filmy pieces of lingerie. "Hank is your client. I don't expect you to discuss your case with me."

"There is something I need to ask you."

"What?"

Rafe picked up the beaded bag. It was bigger than his palm and the variegated rows of coral, gold and white beads rendered the sides as hard as a real clamshell. "Are you positive the bracelet Mercedes had on when you found her was identical to the one Ellen Bishop wore last night at the silent auction?"

Angling her chin, Allie shot him a cynical look. "What, you think I don't know jewelry?"

Pure reflex had him flicking a finger against one of her earrings, sending it swinging. "I suspect you own enough of the pricey stuff to open a jewelry store. So if you tell me you're positive about what bracelet Mercedes was wearing, I'll know for sure."

When he pulled his hand back, his fingertip grazed her cheek. Instantly, a tension as old as Adam and Eve settled in the air. Rafe stood, motionless, gazing down at the woman he was fast becoming unable to resist while his mouth went dry and his gut clenched.

Dammit, he wanted her. So badly his teeth ached. So badly that if she gave him any sign that she wanted him, too, he'd shove all those garment bags and pieces of silk and satin off the table and take her right there.

He watched nerves rush across her face before she dropped her gaze back to the worktable. With grim satisfaction, he noted a slight trembling in her hands when she reached for a peach-colored teddy. At least he wasn't the only one that touch had gotten to.

"When I found Mercedes dead, she was wearing the gold bracelet with heart-shaped diamonds," Allie said as she examined the teddy's side seams. "I'm sure of it." In the next instant, she looked up, awareness snapping into her eyes. "It just occurred to me she had that bracelet on when I saw her earlier that same day."

"Where?"

"Here." Allie laid the teddy aside. "In fact, I was standing at this very table, going over these items with my head seamstress. They're for Katie Jones's trousseau."

Rafe pictured the thin-as-a-shoestring young woman from last night's auction. "Why did Mercedes come here?"

"She'd made some new sketches for her evening bag line and wanted to discuss them with me. When she arrived, she was in a rush because she'd just gotten a call from her lover, who told her he was taking her to Paris that night." Allie shrugged. "That would have been Hank Bishop."

"Yeah." Rafe opened the clamshell-shaped bag. Its satin

lining was snow-white and looked as soft as a cloud. "Did Mercedes have an office here?"

"No, she wasn't an employee. She just designed evening bags, including the one you're holding. If I liked her designs, I bought all rights to them. Usually when I saw Mercedes it was at my shop. And she didn't come here that last time solely to deliver her designs. She'd called and said she wanted to take the lingerie she had on order with her to Paris. I told her the only way her things would be ready was if she came here for a fitting. That way, I could have one of my seamstresses do the final alterations. Before Mercedes rushed out, she promised she would pick up her order from the shop that evening."

"When she didn't show up, you wound up delivering it and found her dead."

"That's right."

Rafe snapped the beaded purse closed and laid it on the table. "When you looked around here today, did you find anything out of place? Something that's here that shouldn't be?"

"Nothing. Claire and I checked—there just isn't anything *not normal.* It's beyond me why Slater wanted in here." She raked a hand through her hair, leaving it appealingly mussed. "Do you want me to show you around the other floors?"

Rafe shook his head. "I saw a lot of the first floor when I came in. Looks like that's where all the packaging and shipping take place."

"And inspecting. None of my merchandise leaves without a final examination."

"What's on the third floor?"

"The computer equipment. My Web site designer has an office there. The stock is stored upstairs, too."

"If you looked everywhere and nothing seems out of place, I'll take your word for it." He glanced at his watch again. He had no idea what time—or even day—it was in Singapore, but he needed to start tracking down the pilot Hank Bishop had fired. "I've got things I need to check. I'll get with Liz later."

"Look, you don't have to…"

He raised a brow when Allie's voice trailed off. "I don't have to what?"

She closed her eyes for an instant. "Liz," she said, looking up at him. "You don't have to go out of your way later trying to find her."

Leaning against the worktable, he crossed his arms over his chest. "What do you suggest?"

"Come to dinner at Claire and Jackson's. Liz will be there."

"Most hostesses hate having uninvited guests pop in."

"You won't be popping in. Claire suggested I invite you. In the summertime, she serves dinner on her building's roof in her patio garden." Allie's mouth curved. "Jackson and Sam—he's Liz's fiancé—fire up the grill and, according to them, show us women how to cook."

"They do a good job?"

"Yes, but it would go to their heads if we admitted that." She raised a hand, let it drop. "It seems like I remember that your mom is a widow and you go to her house every Sunday for dinner. So, if you still do—"

"My mother's dead. She died while I was in prison."

He watched her go pale. "I'm sorry. I didn't know." She paused, then asked, "Did you get to go to her funeral?"

"I didn't *want* to go. It would have been a sign of disrespect to my mother for me to have stood over her grave wearing handcuffs with a guard breathing down my neck."

He damned himself for the bleak look that settled in Allie's eyes. It wasn't her fault, he knew that. Nor was she to blame for the recurring dream that dragged him back all too frequently to the trapped existence of his cell.

"What happened to you was a mistake," she said fiercely, her blue eyes glistening with tears. "A horrible one." She pulled in a shaky breath. "Rafe, how much were you told about why Nina recanted her testimony against you?"

"Not a lot. According to my lawyer, she'd been seeing some psychiatrist. During a session, it came out that she'd repressed memories of her stepfather sexually abusing her. That's who raped her, not me."

Allie nodded. "Her therapist theorized that since you and Nina had just become intimate, being with you had somehow fused with memories of the sexual abuse by her stepfather that she'd suppressed for years. After you brought her home from your date that night, she jerked awake out of a nightmare. All she could remember was she'd been raped. And to her it seemed like it had happened recently."

Allie wrapped her arms around her waist as the old memories settled into her stomach, hard and aching. "Nina woke me up, screaming. I found her huddled on the corner of her bed. She was chalk-white and hysterical. She kept sobbing that she'd been raped. By *you*. I got her to the E.R., and they examined her and called the police. I told the officer what she'd said. They went to your apartment—"

"And hauled me off in front of the entire neighborhood."

It was all Allie could do not to flinch against the hardness in his voice. "I told the police what Nina said. I thought it was the truth. That doesn't make up for what you suffered— I know that." She shoved an unsteady hand through her hair. "If I could, I would try to make up the years you lost."

His throat went tight at the sight of the anguish in her face. "I don't *want* you to try. I don't want…" *You,* he tried to force himself to say the word, but couldn't.

Because she twisted him in knots and he did want her. Viciously. And if he didn't get out of there, he was going to reach for her again and do a lot more than just kiss her.

"You're not to blame for what happened to me." Just by voicing the words, he felt an easing of the tension that had festered inside of him for years. Maybe, just maybe, he'd someday be able to put that vicious, black part of his past totally behind him.

For now, all he wanted was time to get his system under control.

"I've got some things I need to do," he repeated, while sweeping his hand toward the garment bags. "Do you need help carrying those somewhere?"

"No, thanks. I'll manage."

He gazed down into her gorgeous, expressive face. He had spent years rebuilding himself, walling off what little emotion prison hadn't managed to scour away. Yet in this finger-snap of time, he felt himself falling into something with her that he was ill-equipped to handle, didn't want. But hell if he could stay away from her for long.

A dark sense of inevitability settled around him as he scrubbed a hand over his stubbled jaw. Why or how she had swept across the distance he had purposely established between himself and everyone in his life, he didn't know. He just knew she had.

He was going to have to figure out how to deal with that, which meant he needed some space.

"I'll get back to you about dinner," he said, then headed for the door.

* * *

Standing in Claire's kitchen with the scent of simmering apples and cinnamon heavy in the air, Allie slid mushrooms the size of golf balls onto a skewer. Over the faint hum of the air conditioner she heard the clock in the old brick tower that stood in the center of Reunion Square bong six times.

"Rafe won't show up," she said. "After my bringing up his poor, dead mother this afternoon, I don't blame him."

"It's not your fault the woman died while he was in prison," Liz pointed out from the opposite side of the kitchen. Because she barely knew her way around a stove, Claire had assigned her wine-serving duty.

"Diaz told you he needed to talk to me," Liz continued, pulling glasses out of a cabinet. "He didn't drop by the station. He hasn't called." She inclined her head toward the cell phone clipped to the waistband of her pink capris. "Meaning he plans to show up here."

"He could call you later." Allie laid the full skewer in the dish of marinade Claire had prepared.

"Yeah, but my honed detective's instincts tell me he'll ring the doorbell anytime now." Instead of her usual braid, Liz had opted to let her auburn hair flow free over her shoulders and down her back.

"I agree." Claire, clad in a sleek sundress in eye-popping yellow, backed away from the open refrigerator, a platter of thick steaks clenched in both hands. "Rafe will be here."

Allie snatched up an empty skewer, stabbed a mushroom onto it. "I shouldn't have even invited him. I don't know what I was thinking."

"I can guess." Claire set the platter on the counter, then turned to Allie. "You were thinking about that kiss in your office. He knocked your socks off. It's only natural you'd want to find out what will happen after another one."

"Whoa." Liz halted halfway through stripping the foil off the neck of a bottle of straw-colored wine. "What kiss? And how come I haven't heard about it?"

Allie slid Claire a withering look before shifting to face Liz. "If you'd have met us at the warehouse, I'd have told you the same time I told Claire. Bottom line is, Rafe kissed me. I kissed him back. Then we agreed it had been a bad idea."

"Why?" Liz asked. "His 'knocking your socks off' sounds like chemistry wasn't the problem."

If there'd been any more chemistry on her part, steam would have risen through her pores, Allie thought as she impaled another mushroom. Rafe was a different matter. She had seen the way his eyes shuttered when he broke off the kiss, the way he retreated from the intimacy. She had no idea how their close encounter had affected him. *If* it had.

"It's not like Rafe and I stood there, telling each other our reasons why we thought the kiss was a bad idea. But I imagine there's no way he can forget I testified for the prosecution during his trial. For myself, I'm not interested in getting involved in a romantic relationship. Ever."

"Yeah, well, those might be famous last words." Liz took the wine opener and extracted the cork. "I was determined to stay free and single, too, after I broke off my engagement to Andrew. Then Sam walked into my office out of the blue. We're getting married in two months. So much for grand plans."

"Don't forget, Jackson and I had baggage from the past, too," Claire said while digging a barbecue fork and spatula out of a drawer. "I never expected him to show back up in my life." As usual, just talking about the man she loved had

Claire's brown eyes shining and her golden skin glowing. "Jackson was the one for me. I didn't want to admit that at first. Turns out, it was impossible to resist something that was meant to be."

"Not to mention that the best of intentions go down the tubes when there's a hunk involved in the equation," Liz chimed in. "I've seen Diaz up close, Al. Faced with all that broody sexiness, it's no wonder you want to jump his bones."

Allie whipped around from the counter to face her friends. "I don't want to jump…" She trailed off, undone by their patient gazes. "Okay, I admit it. I liked kissing Rafe. I wouldn't mind doing it again. But if we were to sleep together, it would just be sex. That's it. I won't let it be more."

She cut herself off, squeezed her eyes tight. "I felt something. Some sort of connection I've never felt with another man. It scared me. I don't want to take a chance."

"And wind up like your parents," Liz observed. She poured wine in three glasses, passed them around. "It's no wonder you feel that way when all you saw while growing up was relationships crashing and burning. Heck, anyone who'd had five stepmothers would feel the same. But take a look at Claire and Jackson. Then there's Sam and me. We've beat the odds."

"I consider you guys the exception."

Sympathetic, Claire squeezed Allie's arm. "You and Rafe could be, too."

Allie sipped her wine. Willed her system to steady. It was time to refocus her thoughts and just enjoy being with her friends.

She put some effort into making her lips curve. "Anyway, all the talk about Rafe is a moot point. He's not going to show up tonight."

Just then, the doorbell rang.

Rafe jabbed his finger a second time at the bell beside the door of Claire Castle's antique shop. It wasn't the prospect of a few hours socializing on the building's rooftop garden with Allie's friends that had his shoulders tight with tension. It was spending time with *her,* now that he accepted she had managed to find a weakness in the emotional wall he'd thought impervious.

But find it she had, and he intended to figure out what to do about it.

About her.

She was no longer the shallow party girl he'd known in college. He couldn't claim to have a total understanding of her yet, but he was beginning to uncover all those layers and contrasts that made her who and what she was.

Granted, he wanted her physically, but it was much more than that. He was intrigued by her transformation, which fueled an innate curiosity deep inside him to find out how and why the change had come about.

When the door to the shop opened and his gaze settled on Allie, an instant, primal zing of need shot through his gut.

Oh, yeah, he was definitely going to have to figure out what to do about her.

She gazed up at him, her coral-glossed lips forming a cynical curve. "Now that you've shown up, Liz is going to be impossible to live with."

His gaze swept down her, then up. She'd changed into black shorts and a sleeveless top in some sort of floaty material the color of ripe plums. Her bare toes peeked out from under the plum-colored leather tops of a pair of sexy, backless slides. Her hair hung loose in a waterfall of golden blond.

Wanting more time to appreciate the view, he propped a shoulder against the doorjamb. "Why is my showing up going to affect Liz?"

"Because you didn't call or contact her at the station, her honed detective skills told her you were going to show up tonight. And here you are."

He shrugged. "If you want to deflate her ego, I can take off now."

In the moment of electric stillness that followed, he was excruciatingly aware of Allie's well-toned body, the heat and lean curves. Suddenly, he knew how it would be if they slept together…the rise of her hips beneath his, the softness of her flesh against his palms. The last thing he wanted to do was leave.

"You could go," she agreed, looking up at him through thick lashes. "But I don't want to trample Liz's ego, so you'd better stay." She paused for an instant. "I'm glad you're here, Rafe."

She moved back, pulling the door open wider. When he stepped inside, her subtle, sophisticated scent drifted over him like a gentle stroke of hands, making him ache.

The ache didn't lessen when they walked through the cozy shop filled with antiques that glowed in the light of lamps turned low. Or when he followed the gentle sway of her hips up the stairs and stepped into a spacious apartment that brimmed with furniture, paintings and bright rugs that pooled color over the polished wood floor.

"Claire and Liz just headed to the roof to make sure Jackson and Sam have fired up the grill," Allie said as she led him into the kitchen, the heels of her sexy shoes clicking against the floor as she moved. "We'll follow after I get you something to drink. I'm having wine. Would you like some?"

"I lean more toward the soft stuff." In the five years since he'd walked out of prison, he'd made a point to avoid everything that had the potential to affect his control. He'd been successful, except when it came to her. "Tonic with lime will do."

"Coming right up."

Minutes later, they scaled another flight of stairs and stepped out onto the flat rooftop, rimmed with a wrought iron railing. While the sun dipped below the city's skyline, Rafe took in the thickly cushioned patio chairs and small tables placed on a bright all-weather area rug. Bordering the rug were pots brimming with flowers that burst in wild color and filled the air with their scent. A round, glass-topped dining table sat loaded with plates, silverware and glasses.

He slid a hand into the pocket of his khakis. "Impressive."

"It is," Allie agreed. "Claire fashioned it after a restaurant in Paris that she and Jackson visited. When it comes to decorating and setting a scene, she has a gift."

"That she does."

Allie smiled up at him. "Come on, I'll introduce you to Jackson and Sam."

Over the next few hours, Allie didn't relax. How could she when everything female inside her sensed that something about Rafe had changed? She couldn't put her finger on what the change was. It just seemed that whenever his dark gaze settled on her, it felt something akin to a caress. And although he didn't once touch her, she had the unnerving feeling he was crowding her space.

By the time dessert was served, the waxing moon cast a silvery sheen over the rooftop. A soft breeze carried the scent of the potted flowers. And her nerves were wound so tight she felt like a coiled spring.

She slid her gaze sideways. Rafe sat in the chair beside hers, looking totally at ease in the combined glow of moonlight and flames from the candles that sat in the table's center. He even seemed to be enjoying the verbal sparring match Liz had started in an attempt to ferret out details about what Hank Bishop had told him concerning his relationship with Mercedes MacKenzie.

"Come on, Diaz, you're not a lawyer," Liz pointed out while wagging her dessert fork in Rafe's direction. "There's no concept of privilege between a PI and a client. Meaning, if you have information pertinent to the role your client played in Mercedes McKenzie's murder, you're free to tell me."

"True," Rafe agreed as he polished off his apple pie. "However, the retainer my client pays makes it clear where my loyalties lie. By the way, Bishop didn't kill his mistress."

Just then, his cell phone rang. After checking its display, he excused himself from the table and moved to an area of the roof where he wouldn't be overheard.

"He's apparently one PI you aren't going to be able to pry information out of," Sam Broussard said from his chair next to Liz's. The faint, cultured hint of Louisiana in his voice drifted on the warm night air.

"Yeah." Liz sent her fiancé a sly grin. "But it's always fun to try."

Sam reached for her hand, his eyes staying on hers while he pressed a kiss against her palm. "Always," he agreed.

From where she sat across the table, Allie watched her

friend's grin transform into a dreamy smile. Which looked identical to Claire's expression as she sat beside Jackson, their fingers linked.

A flash of emotion shot through Allie, and it took her a moment to realize what she felt was an odd little twist of envy. For the first time ever, she found herself wanting the type of relationship her two friends had with the men in their lives. But finding that kind of forever love involved risk. From what she had seen growing up, she knew all too well that the odds heavily favored unhappy endings.

"Here's something about my case I will share," Rafe said when he returned to the table. He stood behind his chair, resting his hands on the top of its back.

Allie found herself watching his hands in the candlelight. Noting how solid, strong and long-fingered they seemed. Imagining those olive-skinned hands creating havoc on every inch of her naked body was enough to make the muscles in her belly quiver. With her throat as dry as the Sahara, she reached for her wineglass, took a steadying sip.

"I just spoke to the pilot my client fired. He admitted that before he left for the Orient, he told Ellen Bishop about her husband's affair with Mercedes McKenzie. The pilot even picked up McKenzie once and drove her to the airport, so he gave Ellen Bishop the address of McKenzie's condo."

Liz pursed her mouth. "Ellen Bishop being the woman who got snockered last night and tried to put out Allie's lights with a line drive using a Mercedes McKenzie evening bag."

"You got it," Rafe said. "With that kind of anger and strength, she could have easily strangled her husband's mistress. And slugged Allie in the head. In my opinion, your fellow officers arrested the wrong person for the murder. They might want to take a hard look at Ellen Bishop."

"They might," Liz said, her expression unreadable. "But you're still a long way from getting your client off the hook."

"Have to start somewhere." Rafe shifted his attention to Allie, his black-as-midnight eyes locking on hers. "Because everyone except myself pitched in on making dinner, I told Claire I'd do kitchen duty."

Allie arched a brow. "You did?"

"He did," Claire said, raising her wineglass to salute. "I accepted."

He looked back at Allie. "Want to keep me company?"

"Sure." Even as she tossed her hair back in a careless gesture, Allie felt a frisson of anticipation. Maybe by spending some one-on-one time with Rafe she'd get a handle on why her senses screamed that the dynamics between them had changed. "I'm always up for watching a man slave in the kitchen," she added.

"Good." His slow smile, the first real one she'd ever gotten from him, caused her heart to thud.

She picked up her wineglass again. Just as quickly, set it down without taking a drink.

There wasn't enough wine on earth to calm her jangling nerves.

Chapter 9

Never in a million years would Allie have thought there could be anything sensual about watching a man load a dishwasher. But there was something about the way Rafe's impressive muscles rippled beneath his short-sleeved polo shirt while he slid plates into the bottom rack. The limber motion of his hips in nicely fitting slacks, his overall economy of motion had her thinking of a really good golf swing. Or other physically skillful activities.

She took a sip of the ice water she'd switched to after she and Rafe left the other two couples lingering over after-dinner coffee in the rooftop garden. The cool liquid did nothing to soothe the tightness in Allie's throat. How could it when she was certain the dynamics between her and Rafe had changed? The fact she couldn't put her finger on exactly what that change was—or why it had come about—had her tangled nerves feeling tight beneath her skin.

"It was nice of you to volunteer for kitchen duty," she said while drying one of the wineglasses Rafe had washed by hand. "Not every dinner guest would do that."

He added a handful of flatware to the dishwasher's basket. "I believe in pulling my weight."

She placed the glass in a cabinet, wondering how weighty all those powerful muscles, those massive shoulders would feel on top of her.

Aware that her thoughts had trespassed into unsafe territory, she gave herself a mental shake. Plucking another wineglass out of the drainer beside the sink, she went to work with her dish towel and changed the subject.

"So, after talking to the pilot, you now have proof Ellen Bishop knew her husband was having an affair with Mercedes. And Ellen had the address of the condo where Mercedes was murdered. Is that going to help your case?"

"Too soon to tell." Rafe glanced up while positioning the last of the dinner plates in the dishwasher. "Just because Hank Bishop's wife knew he was messing around doesn't mean she did anything about it. And it doesn't mean she didn't."

Rafe grabbed a dish towel and leaned against the counter while drying his hands, his expression thoughtful. "One problem is that if it was Joe Slater she called from the auction last night, I may never be able to prove it."

The mention of the man who had probably broken into her shop, lured her to her warehouse, then tried to run down Rafe sent a chill up Allie's spine. She stowed the last of the wineglasses in the cabinet. "Why not?"

"According to Liz, he had two cell phones. The one clipped to his belt came with him when you and I dragged him out of his burning car. The other was on the passenger seat and melted in the fire. About all the lab techs could tell about the destroyed phone was that it was the cheap type sold at convenience stores. You don't need to subscribe to a service because the phone has prepaid minutes already loaded into it. When that time runs out, you toss the phone."

"Does that mean there are no records to show who calls come from or are made to?"

"Exactly. And because Slater's phone melted, it's not possible to get its own number out of it. If he used it to call you, we'll never be able to prove it. And even if the police had reason to get a warrant to look at Ellen Bishop's cell records, they might show she made a call to a prepaid phone, but there won't be a way to tie the number to Slater."

Allie folded her dish towel and laid it on the counter. "That doesn't sound like good news for your client."

"It depends. Because of what the pilot told me, the police might decide to look a little harder at Ellen Bishop. Maybe recheck her alibi for the night of the murder." Rafe shrugged. "It's always possible they might find a hole there."

"What *is* her alibi?"

"I don't know. Ellen wasn't in the mood at the auction to tell me, and Liz isn't saying. But even if Ellen has an ironclad alibi, she still could have hired Slater to murder Mercedes."

"With Ellen not talking and Slater dead, is your investigation at a standstill?"

"Maybe, maybe not. I have a couple of other things to check out." He snagged a lone fork off the counter, added it to the dishwasher. Holding the door open, he swept his gaze around the kitchen. "See anything else that needs to go in here?"

"No." Allie raised a brow as she studied the dishwasher's

contents. "I've never before seen dishes loaded so that there's not one free inch of space left. That's quite a talent."

"I was assigned kitchen duty in prison."

"Oh." It was amazing, she thought, how flat a man's voice could go in an instant.

Rafe closed the door with a snap. "If I didn't fill the dishwasher the way the guards thought it should be done, I got written up."

A sharp blade of regret had Allie's fingers curling into her palms. "Everything," she said softly. "Your having been in prison affects everything you do. There's no getting away from it, is there?"

"Basically." Rafe stepped toward her, his gaze locked on hers. "Look, I didn't bring up prison just now to make you feel bad. I have a far different reason."

"To remind me you'll never get past the fact I helped send you there?"

"No, although at one time that's pretty much what I believed." He slanted his chin. "When your name first came up in the Bishop case and I realized I'd have to interview you, I wanted to make sure the good-time party-girl understood how much I resented her helping to take two years of my life away over something I didn't do."

"You've made that clear, Rafe. Crystal."

"Which was unfair. And something I've done a lot of thinking about since I first talked to you at your shop." His eyes stayed on hers as he closed the small gap between them. "And you. I've thought a lot about you."

The incredible scent of musky aftershave and potent male surrounded her, making her pulse skip. "What about me?" She hoped her coolly polite tone belied the renewed tangle of nerves.

"I know who you used to be. I'm beginning to learn who you are now. But…you're different." He skimmed a fingertip along the curve of her jaw, leaving a trail of heat. "Even though I'm good at solving puzzles, I figure it's going to take time to get you figured out."

His voice resonated inside her like a tuning fork. "How do you plan to do that?"

"By spending time with you." The steady intensity in his gaze sent a frisson of excitement along every nerve ending in her body. "There's something about you, Allie. Something that's gotten to me. I wasn't looking for that to happen with any woman, certainly not with you. It isn't a comfortable feeling for me, and I've tried my best to shake it. But it's there, so I need to deal with it."

He skimmed a hand down her bare arm until he reached the tight curl of her fingers. Silently he lifted her hand, running his thumb over her knuckles. "I'd like to get to know you better. *This* you, the real you."

The kitchen seemed to fade away. Her entire focus and awareness were on Rafe. She could hear her own pulse in her ears, feel the frantic rush of blood through her veins. "You might not like the present me any more than you liked the old me."

"Not likely."

"Look, Rafe, I…don't do relationships." His touch had kicked her heart into an urgent beat and she could barely get the words out around the tightness in her throat. "I just…don't."

"You don't do relationships. I'm not at all sure I want one. We ought to get along fine."

Temptation had never been greater. Or as appealing. Or as arousing. Which was the reason an alarm now blared in

Allie's head. She wanted him. Wanted to let go of the caution learned from watching her parents' futile quest for happiness and just see what developed.

When his thumb brushed against the pulse point in her wrist, her breath hitched and she could feel herself melting, like a candle left too long in the Oklahoma summer sun. To shore up her resolve, she reminded herself of the feeling that gripped her when he'd kissed her. She had never felt that type of connection to another man and she knew instinctively if she dived into an affair with Rafe, she wouldn't come out of it unscathed.

"We could take things slowly," he suggested. "See how we get along." His hand slid around the back of her neck. His thumb stroked the side of her throat as he lowered his head. "I already know how we get along when it comes to this."

She felt a low tightening in her stomach as his mouth wandered to the edge of her jaw, the corner of her lips.

"We decided kissing each other was a mistake," she managed.

His lips grazed hers. "I'm rethinking my position on that."

The remembered taste of him sent a shudder of pleasure through her. His slow kiss explored without demand while his hand moved to cradle the side of her face. Disarmed by his gentleness, she let her body relax against his.

Closing a hand on her hair, he held it aside and kissed her neck, taking forever to work his way up to the hollow behind her ear. By the time he had reached it, she was twisting to get closer to him, her fingers gripping the unyielding surface of his upper arms.

"Have dinner with me tomorrow night." His warm breath against her cheek had her heart pumping as if she'd run a marathon.

She struggled to think. "I can't. I have…work for the foundation to do."

Just then, the sound of voices drifted from the living room into the kitchen.

Rafe stepped back, his eyes staying steady on hers as he leaned against the counter. "Sounds like your friends are done with their coffee."

"Yes." Allie took a deep breath. The flesh on her throat where he'd trailed kisses felt flushed and tender, as if she'd been scalded.

"You're busy tomorrow," he said quietly. "What about the following night?"

Inside she felt hot. Twisted. And, she admitted, scared as hell. Not of Rafe, but of the power of her own reaction to him. She had to think, had to. But right now she could only feel.

"I don't know." The husky unevenness in her voice made it sound as if someone had attacked her vocal cords with sandpaper. She shoved an unsteady hand through her hair. "This is all so…sudden. I don't know what to say."

"It took me by surprise, too. You don't have to say anything right now. Just let me know about Tuesday night. Okay?"

"I will." She was aware of the sound of Claire and Liz's voices growing louder as her friends neared the kitchen. Maybe by the time they walked in, she'd have her breathing back under control.

Maybe not.

Lord, she needed to think.

She gazed into Rafe's face, his mesmerizing dark eyes, and felt that strange pull toward him. The man had *"dangerous"* written all over him.

Allie pressed a hand to her thundering heart. "As soon as I know, you'll know."

* * *

Rafe spent part of the following morning coaxing information out of a snooty clerk at an exclusive jewelry store. The facts he learned about the diamond bracelet Hank Bishop had left there for repair sent Rafe back to his client's office. There, he dug through the real estate investment company's cell-phone records.

By late afternoon, Rafe was sure Bishop's son had lied to him when they'd spoken at the silent auction, and he wanted a face-to-face with Will Bishop to see his reaction to the evidence. Since Junior had called in sick to work that day, Rafe left several messages on his cell phone. When they weren't returned, Rafe swung by Will's townhouse. There was no answer when he rang the bell and no sign of the man's red sports car.

Rafe finally spotted the car that evening in the parking lot of a trendy club Will Bishop was known to frequent. Before Rafe could get through the main door of The Blues, he had to pay a twenty-dollar cover charge. After being advised of the two-drink minimum, he stepped into the bar area where the sound system oozed earthy, mellow blues.

The sweet scent of marijuana floated on air thick with smoke. Fashionably thin women in clingy summer dresses swayed in the arms of their partners. Bishop, his golden tan and sun-streaked hair giving him the look of a professional surfer, sat at a table chatting up a sloe-eyed blonde wearing a strapless salsa-red dress that fit her body like a good paint job.

As he wove his way closer to the table, Rafe thought about the leggy redhead who'd hung on Will's arm at the silent auction. Junior indeed had an eye for the women.

Still, neither the redhead nor tonight's blonde could touch Allie Fielding when it came to class. Sexiness. Allure.

That sudden, unbidden thought had Rafe frowning. Last night, he'd taken a step with her that would have ramifications he knew he might not be able to handle smoothly. But handle them he would, no matter how she got to him.

Right now, the fact she hadn't yet called to tell him she would—or wouldn't—have dinner with him the following night had his insides churning. He didn't want to acknowledge that her silence bothered him. But, dammit, it did. And he was going to have to figure out what to do about it if she didn't call.

Knowing she could throw him off-balance was far from a comfortable feeling for a man determined to control every aspect of his life.

Rafe was nearly at the table before Bishop glanced his way. Recognition flickered in his eyes, followed by a frown.

"Diaz, can't take a hint? If I wanted to talk to you, I would have returned one of the messages you left."

"You called in sick to work," Rafe said, infusing concern into his voice. "I thought I'd better check on you." Shifting his gaze to the blonde, Rafe jabbed his fingers into the front pocket of his jeans. "It appears you've made a full recovery."

"Thanks to Triana, here." Bishop nudged aside one of the blonde's dangly earrings that was as long as a finger and settled a kiss on her bare shoulder. "She's taking good care of me, so you can just go on."

"If I 'go on,' you'll be talking to cops instead of me."

Bishop leaned back in his chair, watching Rafe closely. "About?"

"A gold bracelet with heart-shaped diamonds."

The corners of Bishop's eyes tightened. "I don't know what bracelet you're talking about."

"It's a twin to the one your mother owns. The police will probably be able to refresh your memory when they take you in for questioning." Rafe turned to leave just as the current dance music faded.

"Diaz, hold on."

Rafe paused, glanced over his shoulder. "What?"

Bishop sent his date a smile so smooth that Rafe figured it had been practiced before a mirror. "Triana, give us a minute while I conduct business."

Her red-glossed mouth settled into a pout as she rose and tottered past Rafe on flame-red ice-pick heels. A song that was low and bluesy, with a lot of sax flowed out of the club's sound system.

The instant Rafe settled into the chair across the small table from Bishop, a waitress appeared. "There's a two-drink minimum, handsome. What can I get you?"

"Tonic with a wedge of lime. Bring both drinks and my tab when you come back."

After Bishop ordered another round, the waitress moved away. "Okay, Diaz, just what is it you think I know about a diamond bracelet?"

Rafe crossed his forearms on the table. He'd already gone over the facts he could prove and those he couldn't. He didn't intend to let Bishop know he was mostly on a fishing expedition.

"Your dad gave Mercedes McKenzie a gold bracelet with heart-shaped diamonds that's a clone of the one your mother owns. When Mercedes's bracelet needed repair, he took it to Trudeau's. They called what they thought was his cell number when it was ready for pickup."

"Interesting story. What does it have to do with me?"

"Plenty. You shop there, too, so they have your cell number on file. Because your family's real estate company supplies your phone, that number is only one digit different from your father's. Instead of calling him, the clerk screwed up and dialed your phone. When you answered, she said, 'Mr. Bishop?' You naturally said, 'Yes.' Things went from there."

"I don't remember that call."

"The clerk does. She said there was blues music playing in the background. She happens to be a fan, too."

"Good for her."

"She also recalls that when she asked if you wanted to pick up the repaired bracelet or have it delivered to the address on Colony Lane, you opted for delivery. Then you had her verify the house number. Colony Lane, as you know, is the location of the condo your father moved his mistress into."

"None of this sounds familiar," Bishop said just as the waitress reappeared with their orders.

Rafe paid his tab before she left. "Better do something about your faulty memory, Will. I spent most of this afternoon at your dad's office, going through cell-phone records. They verify the date, time and number the clerk jotted on the jewelry store's paperwork when she called and notified Mr. Bishop—namely you—that the bracelet had been repaired."

"Like you said, I shop at Trudeau's, too. Could be she called me about a different matter."

"According to Trudeau's, you haven't left any jewelry there for repair—or made a purchase—in more than six months. So you wouldn't have assumed the clerk was calling about a transaction you'd made there. You're a clever guy, Will. You would have figured out almost immediately she'd meant to call your father."

"Prove it."

"I can't. But I can prove you had enough information to figure out your father was having an affair and you had the address of the condo he'd moved his mistress into." Rafe leaned in. "You found all that out only days before McKenzie was murdered at that same address. Maybe you did some checking. Verified your father put his mistress up in one of his condos, bought her a new car and was paying her bills. That wouldn't have gone over big with you."

Bishop's jaw tightened. "You have no idea what I would have thought."

"I can guess." Rafe took a sip of tonic. "It would have been apparent the relationship was more than a fling. You had no way of knowing if your dad planned to divorce your mother, then marry his mistress. If that happened, she would have a claim to a chunk of his business and maybe all of your inheritance." Rafe raised a shoulder. "The prospect of getting rid of your future stepmother would have been appealing to someone in your shoes."

"Someone in my shoes would have known that murdering the woman would have put my dad's affair in the open. My mother would find out. That was the last thing I wanted."

Tighten that jaw another notch, Junior, something's going to snap, Rafe thought. "Your mother knew about the affair weeks before the murder."

Bishop sat silent for a moment, then shook his head. "I don't believe that. If she'd known, she wouldn't have just stayed quiet and taken it."

Maybe she didn't, Rafe thought.

Bishop leaned in. "I'd already left the auction when

Mother confronted Allie Fielding. But I heard all about it, so I know you witnessed it. My aunt spent all night trying to get my mom settled down."

"Your aunt and your uncle," Rafe corrected, thinking of Guy Jones's comment the previous day when he'd seen him and Hank Bishop at the vacant building.

"Uncle Guy didn't hang around to help out." Bishop drained his glass. "He dropped them off at Mother's house after the event, then went home."

Interesting, that Guy Jones had said just the opposite, Rafe thought. "Are you sure about that?"

"I swung by my mother's house. Uncle Guy had already taken off."

Rafe glanced toward the dance floor where couples swayed to a tune that was earthy and mellow. "Guess I got my facts wrong," he said.

"Not just about my uncle," Bishop said, stabbing an index finger in Rafe's direction. "Bottom line, Diaz, you can accuse me all you want. Make up scenarios about my mother. But neither one of us killed the McKenzie slut. My dad did. Just because you can't get your client off the hook doesn't mean I'll let you put my mother or myself on it."

"Because you're innocent, you shouldn't have a problem telling me where you were when McKenzie was murdered."

Bishop shrugged. "I was with a gorgeous woman."

"Her name?"

"It's none of your business. I don't want you harassing any of my women." Bishop glanced up. "Speaking of which, here comes Triana," he said as his date sashayed toward the table.

Rafe stood. In the morning, he would check back copies of the newspaper's archives. He figured Bishop—and some of his women—would have made the society page. It was possible one of the dates he'd been photographed with could verify if Junior had been with her the entire night of the murder.

Rafe decided to cast a line one last time in the fishing pond. "I've got one more question."

"Make it quick," Bishop said, his gaze tracking the blonde.

"When's the last time you talked to Joseph Slater?"

Bishop's brow furrowed. "The guy who used to be a builder?"

"One and the same."

"I ran into him about a week ago."

"Where?"

"I checked out a piece of property to see if the company wanted to buy it. Slater was looking at it, too."

"To buy himself?"

"He didn't say. If you want to know what Slater's up to, why don't you call him?"

"Maybe I will," Rafe said, then turned from the table. Either Junior was an award-winning actor or he didn't know Slater was dead.

Rafe was in the club's parking lot, winding his way toward his car when his phone rang. He pulled it out of his pocket while he walked, checked the display. And felt his chest tighten when he saw Allie's name.

He leaned against the hood, answered the call.

"I hope I'm not bothering you," she said.

He narrowed his eyes. Was it worry he heard in her voice? "I just finished an interview. What's up?"

"Rafe, I need to talk to you."

"Is something wrong?"

"Yes. At least I think so. But this isn't about me. There's some business I'd like to discuss with you."

"Did something happen at the shop? Or your warehouse?"

"No, it's the foundation's business. Rafe, I need to talk to you about it tonight. In person. I wish I could come meet you, but I'm working the foundation's hotline until ten and can't leave. Could you come here?"

"Sure. Where's here?"

"My house. The calls are routed here on the nights I work the line."

Rafe checked his watch. "I can be there in fifteen minutes."

"Good."

After the call ended, Rafe eased out a breath. He was quickly learning there was more to Allie Fielding than just contrasts and layers. There were complications, too.

The sound of soft music drifted out of the club, settling around him in the murky darkness. He was mildly surprised to realize that the idea of complications didn't make him want to turn around and walk away from the woman.

Instead he wanted to move closer.

Chapter 10

"I can't stop thinking about him dragging me into that van. It's like I can feel his hands on me all over again."

Listening to the caller's distressed voice through the phone's headset, Allie sat in her home office, inputting the woman's pain-filled words into her computer. This was the victim's first call to the Friends Foundation's hotline. If she phoned again, the volunteer who answered could access the foundation's computer system and see the background information Allie was currently compiling.

"Olivia, what you're going through is understandable." The training Allie had received to work with victims of violent crime was so ingrained she no longer had to consciously remind herself to keep her voice calm. Unemotional. "It's going to take time for you to figure out how to deal with what happened to you."

"How much time?" The words came in a trembling

rush. "It's been *three months* since he grabbed me in that dark parking lot. My boyfriend says I should stop thinking about it. Should make myself forget what that guy did to me. I've tried, but I can't. I don't know what to do."

The woman's desperate tears sent a rush of sympathy through Allie. Her friend Nina had dealt with much the same emotions.

"Some victims manage to put what they endured in the back of their minds. Even if you can't, there are ways to cope."

"How?"

"The foundation has therapists available. I can make an appointment for you to talk to one this week."

"I don't have much money. Or insurance."

"We take care of all costs." Allie's fingers skimmed across the keyboard. "All you have to do is to show up for your appointment. We also have group sessions that your boyfriend can attend with you."

"Okay." Olivia inhaled a trembling breath. "I'll show up. I don't know about my boyfriend."

"That's something we can deal with later." Allie skipped to the screen for the appointment log. By the end of the call, a measure of relief sounded in Olivia's voice.

Allie eased her chair back from her heavy, antique desk. She'd converted the entire third floor of her boathouse into a large office. On the wall opposite her desk sat the drawing table where she sketched lingerie designs. Fabric samples filled the built-in drawers that lined one wall. Moonlight poured in the high, wide windows that she'd opened to catch the breeze off the river.

She checked her watch, saw it was just after ten. With her shift now over, she tugged off the headset and shut down her computer. She had manned the hotline long enough to know which callers would follow through getting the help they'd asked for. Olivia was in that column.

The call that had come in earlier from a woman named Dena was altogether different. Totally disturbing. So much so that Allie had made the decision to overlook one of the foundation's hard-and-fast rules. Still, she knew without a doubt that contacting Rafe had been the right thing to do.

The same thing went for the decision she'd made about Rafe.

A decision that had put a constant hollow throb of regret in the pit of her stomach. Although the attraction between them bordered on *scorching,* the past had taught her that emotions burned white-hot for only a time before dying down to ashes.

Best to walk away before either she or Rafe got singed.

Nothing major had happened between them, after all, she reasoned. Okay, kissing him had set her off like a summer brush fire. But the jolt of panic that shot through her had scared the hell out of her. She'd vowed never to let herself feel that kind of connection. She absolutely wasn't going to open herself up that way.

Thank goodness it wasn't too late to back away.

Which was exactly what she intended to do.

Rafe jogged up the front steps of Allie's boathouse and rang the bell. Seconds later, the door swung open.

She wore a red halter top and snug black shorts. Her feet were bare. In the glow of the porch light, he skimmed his gaze along her naked legs, long and tan and soft. Her tousled blond hair framed her face in a ring of gold.

Did she shock every man's system, he wondered, just

the look of her? Or was he simply vulnerable when it came to her? While the subtle scent of her perfume filled his lungs, he decided either answer wouldn't be to his liking.

The worried look in her eyes reminded him why he was there. He'd heard that same worry in her voice when she called.

"You said you have some foundation business to discuss?"

Because her heart had jammed like a fist in her throat, all Allie could do was nod. He looked ridiculously handsome in jeans and a white dress shirt unbuttoned at the throat and folded back from his forearms. The shirt's stark whiteness made his dark eyes seem almost black and gave his olive skin an even more burnished look. Then there were those shoulders that looked mile-wide beneath the starched fabric.

It was as if someone had plunked down a six-foot-three, one-ninety pound package of pure male temptation on her doorstep.

"Thanks for coming," she finally managed, and opened the door wider to let him in. "I know it's getting late."

"Doesn't matter."

While she willed her nerves to settle, she watched his gaze sweep over the living room with its comfortable furniture and bright area rugs. Light from the table lamps illuminated the eclectic mix of prints, posters and mirrors that hung on the walls. In front of the brick fireplace, a pair of creamy sofas faced each other. Here, in this sanctuary she'd created for herself, she'd wanted no reminder of the cold, loveless mansion she grew up in.

The thought was a stark reminder of her decision to close the door on any sort of relationship with Rafe. Even so, it would be easier to stick to her guns if she wasn't breathing in the subtle, woodsy scent of his aftershave.

"How about we talk out on the back deck?" she asked while leading the way down the hallway. "There's a breeze off the river tonight."

"Sure."

"Would you like something to drink?" She paused just inside the door to the kitchen where copper pots hung in descending order of size from a ceiling rack. "Tonic with fresh lime?"

"Sounds fine."

Hoping to shore up her nerves, Allie poured herself a glass of merlot.

On the small wooden deck, they settled in thickly cushioned chairs, separated by a glass-topped end table. Thanks to outdoor lighting and the moonlight, she could make out the river's dark flow and shapes of trees on the opposite shore.

Ice rattled in Rafe's glass as he took a sip of tonic. "So what's on your mind?"

"I know you're busy trying to clear Hank Bishop of the murder charge. But something came up tonight and I have a bad feeling about it."

"I've got some leads to follow, but they can wait until morning. Your instincts are telling you something's wrong. It's never smart to ignore that type of feeling." He inclined his head. "Tell me."

"Okay." Allie tasted her wine, then plunged in. "The foundation maintains a hotline for victims of violent crime. I volunteer one night a week to answer calls, which are routed here. That's what I was doing tonight."

"Am I here because of one of those calls?"

"Yes. There are strict guidelines about the hotline. One being that callers remain anonymous, if that's their preference. A woman named Dena called tonight. Her first name is the only identifying information she would give."

"Go on."

"Her common-law husband drinks and beats her."

"Why doesn't she leave him?"

"She did once. He found her and nearly killed her. He swore if she tried to leave him again, he'd finish the job."

Just thinking about the call chilled Allie's flesh. There'd been no fear in the woman's words, just dull acceptance.

"They have a two-year-old son," she continued. "Dena swore her husband hasn't laid a hand on the boy, but she said he gets furious when the child cries or spills something. She's afraid it's a matter of time before her husband hurts him."

Allie set her glass aside. "I assured her the foundation can protect her and her son. That we'll get them into a shelter where they'll be safe."

"I take it you don't think she's going to leave the guy?"

"No. I got the impression she believes there's no place to hide where he won't find her."

"Not much you can do if she won't get herself and the kid out of there."

"Not officially, which is why I called you instead of Liz." Shifting on the chair's thick cushion, Allie pulled a slip of paper out of her shorts pocket. "Dena called on the landline at her house. The number showed up on caller ID."

Rafe took the paper, glanced at it. "You want me to trace this number, right? Find out who and where she is."

"I want to *hire* you to do that. I'm acting solely as a private citizen, who needs the services of a PI. Dena said her husband has been arrested before and he's on parole."

"If the woman and her son are in imminent danger, Liz

is who you should contact. No matter how you got that phone number."

"The 'imminent danger' is on hold for now. Dena got up the courage to call the hotline because her husband is on a fishing trip with some pals."

"I'll run the number." Rafe slid the paper into the pocket of his shirt. "I can't promise anything, but I'll try to figure out if there's a way to buy her some time to get away from here."

"Thank you, Rafe." Just knowing there might be a way to help Dena had relief seeping through Allie. "I couldn't just sit back and do nothing."

"Understandable." Over the rim of his glass, Rafe studied her. Although he couldn't have said how he knew it, her worry about two people she'd never met came straight from the heart. He knew now there was nothing left of the wild party girl his path had crossed in college.

"You said you spend one night a week answering hotline calls?"

"Saturday nights, usually. Since the silent auction conflicted with that, I traded for tonight."

"Lots of single women keep Saturday nights open for dates."

He saw the instant tensing of her bare shoulders. "I date once in a while, but nothing serious. When I told you I don't do relationships, I meant it." The hand she used to shove back her hair trembled. "While you're here, that's something we should talk about."

Rafe felt the muscles in his own shoulders tense. From the kisses they'd shared, he knew the chemistry was there, on both sides. This woman had twisted his emotions open, shaken the foundation he'd thought unshakable. And if body language was any precursor of the future, she was gearing up to tell him she wasn't interested in seeing him.

He set his glass on the table. "Sounds like I don't need to make a dinner reservation for tomorrow night."

"You don't." Emotion flickered in her eyes. "I'm sorry, Rafe, I just don't think our seeing each other would work."

"You may be right," he said quietly. "But I'm not convinced. I'd like to know why you seem to be."

She broke eye contact with difficulty, while a low whisper in the back of her mind sounded just enough volume to question her decision to end things before either of them were in too deep. What the hell was going on? Emotional attachments didn't last; she knew that on the most basic level. She'd never been foolish enough to let a man get *that* close. Yet now she found the prospect of turning her back on Rafe sent a shiver of deep uncertainty through her. Her heart beat fast and her vision blurred as she looked blindly out at the river's opposite shore.

"It's a long story," she said, keeping her gaze diverted from his. "Stuff I've dragged along from childhood."

When she reached for her wineglass, he closed his hand around hers. "Tell me."

Her hand trembled against his. "I don't like to talk about my past."

"I'd like to know." He entwined his fingers with hers. "To understand."

The tenderness in his touch, his voice, caught Allie off guard. She felt raw inside, stripped of her customary protective layers, which left her vulnerable to this avalanche of unfamiliar feelings.

"Please."

She squeezed her eyes shut against the sudden realization that she *wanted* him to understand what growing up had been like for her. *Needed* him to understand.

"The only memories I have of my parents together are of their constant fighting. When I was five, my mother packed her clothes and moved back to California to try to revive the acting career she'd given up when she married my father. She left without saying goodbye to either of us."

Rafe's thumb slid across her knuckles. "That had to have been rough."

"It was. She was beautiful. Elegant. I used to pretend she was a fairy princess and I would grow up just like her."

"How often did you see her after she left?"

"Never." It still hurt, Allie conceded. No matter how often she told herself it was foolish to allow the pain to grind at her after so long. "She never came back. Never sent for me."

Too on-edge from the memories—and Rafe's touch—to remain seated, she tugged her hand from his, rose and moved to the wooden railing that edged the deck. The river flowed past in murky silence.

"About a month after my mother left, she sent me a letter. In it she explained that her life had become impossible. A total separation was the only way she could be happy. She added that she regretted leaving me, but she couldn't be a good mother."

Behind her, she heard Rafe rise, listened to his footsteps as he moved to stand beside her at the rail, her wineglass dangling from his fingers. "You were five years old. Could you even grasp what she was telling you?"

"The way my mind interpreted it was that she had been miserably unhappy and it was my fault. If I'd been a better daughter, then she wouldn't have been so unhappy and would have stayed. Or at least taken me with her."

Rafe handed her the glass. "How long did it take you to figure out her leaving wasn't your fault?"

"Years. My father had always acted remote toward me, and my mother's leaving didn't change that." Aware of the bitterness in her voice, Allie took a long sip of the bracing wine while making a conscientious effort to rebury the emotion deep inside her.

"I felt awkward and inadequate around him. Even so, he was all I had left and I was terrified he would leave, too. I convinced myself that there was something lacking in me that kept my parents from loving me. So I became the model daughter, always minding the nannies and tutors hired to care for me."

"Did that get any response from your dad?"

"He was never around me long enough to notice." She stared out at the dark water. "He remarried a few months after he divorced my mother. His new wife was French and disliked children. I wasn't allowed at their wedding."

An old, familiar ache settled in Allie's belly. There was no way to explain how lost she had been. How confused she'd felt at seeing her father with another woman as though her mother had never existed.

"That marriage lasted two years. He wed again. Divorced. Some affairs followed. A couple more marriages. Five total. He was engaged again when he died of a heart attack."

"Busy guy."

"Always too busy for me."

She set her glass on the top of the rail, then curled her fingers into her palms. When she'd told Liz and Claire about her childhood, the telling had hurt. Tonight, although she still felt the echo of the old pain, it had been easier to relate the details of her past to Rafe, which was just one more disconcerting fact where the man was concerned.

She shrugged. "Told you it was a long story."

"So you did." He turned his back to the water and leaned against the railing. "No wonder you shy away from relationships."

"Through all those years, a lot of people came into my life. The only ones who stayed were the servants whom my father paid to be there. I don't remember ever seeing him happy with my mother or any other woman. Truly happy."

"So you decided to take the safe approach."

Why did hearing him say what she knew was the truth sound a little too close to cowardice? "What I decided to do was never place my hopes, my needs or my wants in anyone else's hands. My life is just the way I want it. The way I need it to be."

"I thought the same about mine. Then we crossed paths again." He slanted his chin. "When we kissed in the back room of your shop, the attraction was there. It was hot, heavy and it was mutual. Do you agree?"

In the moonlight his face was stronger, more attractive, than it had a right to be. His eyes as dark as the water flowing in the river behind them.

"Yes, the chemistry was there." And if he hadn't pulled back and stopped the kiss, she still wasn't sure she would have. "It *is* there. That doesn't change things."

"The hell it doesn't." When his gaze drifted to her mouth, she felt a jolt of lust. Okay, so maybe it did change things, she admitted. Heart hammering, she looked him square in the eye. "What do you suggest we do about it?"

"Compromise. We see each other, but we get rid of most of the risk."

"How?" The word was almost a plea.

"We take this on a day-to-day basis." He skimmed a fingertip over her jaw. "We go out only if the mood strikes us both." When his finger trailed down the length of her throat, everything inside her turned hot and sensitive. "By the end of the evening, we should know if we want to see each other again. Or not. We take things from there."

She shivered when he whispered the last words over her lips, which were trembling with the need he aroused in her. She tried to catch her breath, to make sense of her response with a mind that felt suddenly numb.

"That sounds...too easy," she said, her voice thready. Why did she have to want him so much? "Like there's a...catch."

"Could be." His hands came to her hips as he spoke, rode up to just under her breasts. His lips brushed over hers, brushed again. "For instance, one of us might want to move faster than the other."

Her hands rose to his chest, her fingers curling into the fabric of his shirt while raw, primal need sprang free inside her. No other man had ever affected her so intensely and on every level. If this thing between her and Rafe had been only physical, she liked to think she would've found it easier to step away as she knew she should. As she'd told herself she *would*. But for her, there was apparently no stepping away from this one man.

"You're moving just fine, Diaz."

His lips curved into one of his rare smiles. "It feels fine to me, too," he said as one of his arms slid around her waist to lock her against him.

And when his mouth lowered to hers, she found herself meeting him.

His kiss was hot. Burning hot. Frankly sexual. Warm,

moist lips meeting hers, open, inviting, offering. He traced his tongue slowly around the edge of her lips, then slipped deeper, probing, exploring. She tried to catch her breath and caught his instead, hot and flavored with the taste of tonic and lime.

The heat flowed down over her, followed by his hands. He ran his palms over her back, chasing shivers, setting off new ones, sliding lower.

She tangled her hands in the silken strands of his black hair and slanted her mouth across his as needs too long ignored sprang to life. Desire swelled inside her, pushing aside sanity, blazing a trail for more instinctive responses. Arching against him, she lost herself in the kiss, in the moment.

His hand streaked over her bottom, kneading, stroking. When his fingertips grazed the bare skin between the hem of her halter top and waistband of her shorts, her throat burned dry.

Even though Rafe hadn't said it out loud, she knew where this was going. And she wanted to go there. She wanted this man more than she'd ever wanted anything in her life.

Rafe's blood pounded a hard primal beat as he gazed down into her vivid blue eyes. She felt lean and warm in his arms, and he wanted her. Against her lips, he murmured, "Should we take this inside?"

She stared up at him for a moment, long enough to have his chest going tight before she whispered, "Yes."

He raked his fingers through her hair. "You're sure?"

In answer, she fused her mouth to his.

"Good enough," he groaned.

Sweeping her into his arms, he carried her across the deck and into the house. Made it through the kitchen to the living room, which was a major accomplishment, considering the way her teeth savaged his throat.

He paused. "Bedroom, couch or floor?"

"Okay."

He shifted and joined their mouths in a deep, mutual exploration that left both of them breathing even harder than before.

"Bedroom," he said finally. "This first time, we need a bed." He craned his neck. "Which way?"

"Upstairs," she panted. "Second floor." One of her hands locked on the back of his neck while the other fought to open the buttons of his shirt. "First...door on...right," she added against his mouth. *"Now."*

"We're going." With her arms wrapped around him like silken rope, he started toward the stairs, ran into the corner of one of the sofas and knocked them both back against the banister.

He muttered an oath. "You okay?"

Her response was to shove his shirt off one shoulder and replace fabric with teeth.

Desperate to feel her, he streaked a hand beneath her halter top. He sent up silent thanks when all he found was hot, bare flesh.

With his hand closed possessively over one soft breast and their mouths fused in a tongue-tangling kiss, he carried her up the staircase, arms and legs banging against the wall. When they surged into the dimly lit hallway at the top of the stairs, Rafe jerked off the halter, pressed her back against the wall and fastened his mouth on one hard, tight nipple, suckling greedily.

Her low, throaty moan filled his senses, as potent and drugging as whiskey.

While he fed on her, she shoved the shirt farther down his arms, then dug her nails into his shoulders. "We aren't…going to make it…to the bedroom," she breathed.

"Don't bet on it." He dragged her away from the wall and took the brunt when they rammed into the bedroom door.

"Hurry." She nipped his jaw, then scraped her teeth down his throat while the word pumped like a pulse in his blood. *Hurry. Hurry.*

They reeled into a bedroom where moonlight streamed through a pair of French doors. He saw the silhouette of a bureau, desk and bookshelf. Beyond them, the sleigh bed was a veritable lake of smooth linens and pillows. Here the scents that were uniquely Allie were stronger than ever; he could smell her smoldering perfume, a cunning female fragrance meant to make a man lose his mind.

It was working.

With her clinging to him like a burr, he crossed the room and tumbled with her onto the bed.

If he'd gone insane with need, so had she. As though in silent agreement, neither gave thought to gentleness, to soft words or slow hands. They tore at each other, kicking off shoes, dragging off clothes while feeding on each other with greedy kisses.

Rising over her, he kneed her thighs apart. He was keenly aware of every inch of her heated flesh, of every soft, supple curve, all there for his exploration and taking. Feeling a primitive need to conquer, to possess, he caught her wrists in one hand and stretched her arms over her head, arching her breasts upward. He dipped his head, suckled.

The feral purr that sounded in her throat went straight to his head like hot whiskey.

Their want of each other, *need* for each other was huge, ruthlessly keen. Right now it was all that mattered.

To please her, and himself, he skimmed his free hand over her belly, down between her spread legs. He cupped her, found her wet and hot and unbearably arousing. Hunger for her pumped inside him. His fingers plunged into her while he gorged himself on her flesh.

Her breath strained as her head tossed restlessly back and forth within the frame of her upstretched arms. When she breathed his name, heat saturated him, as though a furnace door had been thrown open and the roaring blaze enveloped the room.

With his fingers impaling her, he could feel every pulse beat pounding inside her. His thumb circled the bud between her thighs, an erotic massage of her throbbing flesh.

His fingers withdrew, entered her again, then again. Sweat slicked her lush curves; he felt her muscles clench, the spasms boil swiftly upward.

"Again," he murmured. He sensed himself edging toward the boundaries of control while his fingers continued moving inside her. His thumb stroked her flesh until he shot her back up that slippery, heated path.

He swept his jeans off the floor, pulled a foil packet from his billfold.

Her hands settled on his. "Let me."

He gritted his teeth while she sheathed him.

"Now." Her lips trembled. "I want you inside me now."

She held his gaze as he thrust inside her, his heart crashing like thunder. He slid deeper, each move fueled by increasing urgency, increasing greed.

Need tore at him, clouding his mind, his vision. She arched higher to take him in fully, her hips meeting his thrust for thrust as their bodies mated. Her muscles clenched around him at the same moment his body convulsed.

With the earth moving beneath him, he buried his face in the golden fire of her hair and surrendered himself to her.

Chapter 11

The dream jolted Rafe awake.

In his mind, it hadn't been the walls of Allie's bedroom closing in on him but the iron bars of his prison cell. Black, cloying memories twisted his insides into knots. His fingers curled into the sheet. He felt the nausea roll in his stomach, the familiar cold sweat break out on his skin, and the unfamiliar sensation of a woman wrapped around him.

"Are you okay?" she murmured, her voice foggy with sleep.

He bit back a strangled curse that he'd woken her. The last thing he wanted was for her to witness him battling the demon from his past.

"I'm fine," he said through gritted teeth. "Be back in a minute."

He wasn't fine. He'd had the dream often enough to know that trying to reason with the panic that tightened his throat and made his lungs strain was wasted effort. The monster clawing at his insides wasn't going to stop until he got outside where the air was clean and there were no walls caging him in.

Her palm moved against his chest. "Your heart is hammering." She lifted her head. Enough moonlight streamed into the bedroom that he could see the concern in her eyes. "Bad dream?"

"Yeah."

"Anything I can do?"

"I've had it before. I just need some fresh air."

His teeth clamped tight on an oath, he eased away from her. He forced himself to ignore her soft protest, to disregard the silky warmth of her skin that tempted him to tug her back into his arms. He had to get outside. *Now.*

He grabbed his jeans off the floor and jerked them on. Earlier when they'd come up for air, he'd opened the bedroom's French doors that led to the second-floor balcony and spotted a wicker chaise lounge.

That was as good a place as any to wait for the overwhelming wave of claustrophobia that always accompanied the dream to ease.

His bare feet sank into carpet so thick it would muffle the sound of a jack hammer as he moved toward the open doors. Stepping outside, he gripped the railing that ran the length of the balcony. The air he dragged into his lungs was clean and sharp and he couldn't get enough of it. As usual, it took only a few minutes for the panic and grinding nausea to begin to fade.

He scrubbed a hand across his stubbled jaw and turned back toward the bedroom. Allie was on her feet now; in the moon's pale glow, he could see every lush curve of her body. When she bent and swept his white shirt off the floor, the glimpse of her gorgeous backside shot heat to his loins.

That his body reacted to her while he was still trying to shake off the remnants of the dream was testimony to the hold she already had on him. He warned himself that he was rapidly approaching quicksand. A few more steps and he could end up in over his head. If he wasn't already there.

A disquieting thought for a man used to having a handle on himself and the world around him.

Except for the damn dream.

He settled on the cushioned chaise lounge. Easing his head back, he took a series of long, deep breaths while watching the big moon skim in and out of fat gray clouds. It had been five years since he'd been locked in a cell. *Five years.* Yet, each dream dragged him back to that trapped existence, making it seem so real that even the clang of the cell door sliding shut behind him echoed in his head.

"I brought you some water."

Allie stood beside the lounge, her hair a golden tangle around her shoulders. The hem of his white dress shirt skimmed her soft-as-silk thighs.

She looked sexy and decadent.

"Thanks." He accepted the glass; the cool water felt like heaven against his parched throat. "Sorry I woke you."

"I'm sorry you had a bad dream." Her hand settled on his shoulder, squeezed. "Do you want to be alone?"

Knee-jerk reflex put the word *yes* on the tip of his tongue. Yet her touch moved something deep inside him, and in a heartbeat of time, he felt himself take another step toward that quicksand.

At that instant, he couldn't make himself care.

"Company would be good." He set the glass on the floor

then reached up and snagged her wrist. "As long as you don't mind staying out here for a while."

"I don't mind, as long as you share the lounge."

"Deal." Shifting his legs wide, he tugged her down so that her bottom settled in the V of his thighs. "Lean back," he said. "Use me for a cushion."

She rested her spine against his bare chest, then propped her head against his shoulder. "Nice cushion," she murmured.

"Nice body," he commented, wrapping his arms around her waist. Spooning, he thought, had never felt so good.

One of her hands rested on his. "Want to tell me about the dream?"

"No."

"That was my answer earlier when you asked if I wanted to talk about my childhood. I wound up telling you because you said you'd like to know."

He felt the soft tickle of her hair against his cheek, smelled its dark, sensual scent. "Are you trying to make this a quid pro quo deal?"

"You said you've had the dream before. That means something's bothering you." Just as he'd done earlier when he coaxed her to talk to him, she entwined her fingers with his. "I'd like to know what it is. To understand." Her thumb glided over his knuckles. "To help, if I can."

It was amazing, he thought, that the child raised by cold, distant parents had become a woman who put her time and her money into helping crime victims. Her down-to-earth basic kindness drew him with the same force as her compelling smile and sexy curves. Was it any wonder that with every layer he uncovered he felt even more in-trigued? More intent on getting to the heart of who she was.

More determined to keep her in his life, which by his own design, had been solitary and emotionally sterile.

That he now found himself longing for something more hit him harder than any punch he'd ever taken. He was not going to be able to stay out of the quicksand with Allie Fielding.

That he had no clue how the hell to handle that was just one more thing to think about.

He curled his fingers around hers. "In the dream I'm back in prison, locked in my cell," he began, intent on giving her a watered-down version. "The air is so thick and heavy I can barely breathe. I hear the clang of the door sliding shut, trapping me. I'm locked up again. With no way out."

"That must be awful."

"Not pleasant." The wrenching sadness in her voice tightened his chest. "I figure someday it'll stop. Until then, I spend a lot of time outside at night."

"Have you thought about seeing a therapist? Someone who can try to figure out how to make the dream stop?"

"I'd rather do some more figuring out about you."

She shifted her head to look up at him. "Didn't my telling you about my childhood do that?"

"Not entirely." It was his turn to slick his thumb across her knuckles. "You left off where your being a model daughter didn't get your father's attention. It's my guess that by the time you got to college, you decided to change tactics. If sterling behavior couldn't catch his eye, making waves might. And that wave-making young woman is who I crossed paths with."

With her bottom nuzzled against his loins and her back plastered against his hard-as-granite chest, Allie's system was already jittery. The steady glide of his thumb across

her knuckles ramped up her nerves even more so that she
had to struggle to focus on his words.

Oh, boy, she thought. Oh, boy. The ground was a lot
shakier than she'd anticipated. Granted, the hot blood and
frenzied passion of their first time together had rocked her
world. But that dimmed in comparison with the tenderness
he had shown her after that. The memory of the passion
she'd felt in his touch, the soft words he'd whispered against
her heated flesh had her body going weak all over again.

Surely everything inside her felt so intensified because
of the emotional whirlwind that came from telling him
about her past, not to mention sleeping with him.

Feeling vulnerable to this avalanche of unfamiliar feelings, she decided what she was dealing with was lust. Lust
deluxe. Lust was something she could handle. Lust was
manageable.

Lust did not rip out one's heart.

"You're right," she said, forcing herself to focus on his
last comment. "I stopped studying. Hung with a wild crowd
and never missed a party. Chose totally inappropriate boyfriends. Spent lavishly on clothes, cars and jewelry."

"Did any of that do the job?"

"Not in the way I wanted," she said, feeling a distant,
dull ache of regret. "When I got picked up for unpaid parking tickets, my father sent his attorney to deal with things.
If I maxed out my credit cards, his accountant showed up.
It didn't matter what I did or how I acted, my father chose
to deal with me from a distance."

"And all you really wanted was him."

"Yes." She raised a shoulder. "Through it all, he continued having affairs, getting married, divorced. He didn't
even send word to me about his last marriage. I found out

about it when I saw the announcement in the paper. Same thing goes for when he divorced that wife."

"What about your mother? Did you ever hear anything about her?"

"Just that she died two years before my father."

Rafe pressed a kiss against her hair. "I'm sorry."

"So am I." Pushing away the age-old regrets, she snuggled deeper into his arms. Against her bottom, she felt him harden. Her mouth curved. "So, Diaz, you've heard all about my past. Happy now?"

"Getting there." The husky timbre of his voice reminded her of how it felt to lie in his arms, he inside her. The memory sent heat swarming into her blood.

"Better get there fast," she murmured.

"I've got one more question." His fingertips brushed against her throat when he nudged her hair back. "What happened to make the ultimate party-girl do an about-face? Must have taken something big for you to establish a foundation, start designing lingerie and open a shop."

The question instantly cooled the fire in her blood. She scooted sideways so she could see his face. "You may not want to hear the answer."

His forehead furrowed. "Why? Does it involve some guy?"

"It has to do with Nina. And what happened to you."

She saw the shutter come down, leaving his expression unreadable. "I'm listening."

"Her father worked for years as the gardener on our estate. That's how Nina and I met and became best friends. The only times we weren't together were the weekends she spent with her mother and stepfather. Nina and I told each other everything. At least I thought we did."

Allie gathered Rafe's hand in hers. "She never told me her stepfather molested her. If only she had, maybe she wouldn't have repressed the memories. Never woken up that night, knowing she'd been raped, but naming you instead of her stepfather."

Rafe's gaze shifted to the dark, distant river. "I learned a long time ago that 'if only's' are a waste of time."

"They are," Allie agreed quietly. "About six months after your trial, Nina started having nightmares. Over time, she drew into herself. Her grades took a nosedive." Allie shook her head. "She was attending college on a full scholarship, and she just stopped going to class.

"One night, she paced the living room of our apartment for hours while she cried. She was literally falling apart before my eyes and I was terrified she would try to kill herself."

Rafe's gaze whipped back to meet hers. "Did she?"

"I didn't give her the chance. I called my father and got the unlisted number of his golf buddy who was a big-time therapist. The doctor had a year-long waiting list for new patients, but I begged him to see Nina. I had to drag her to his office at first.

"After a while, he got her to join group sessions with other female crime victims. Nina asked me to go with her for support, so I did. The therapist saw how shaky she was, so he allowed me to sit in on the sessions, too. I sat and listened. Just listened. Some of the women struggled to just get through each day. For me, that was the final dose of reality. I started thinking about the direction my own life was headed. After a while, I accepted that no matter what I did, my father would never love me. That I was wasting time, energy and money trying to make the impossible happen."

Allie eased out a breath. Even now, she felt the relief

that had come with that acceptance. "There were people who *did* need something I could give them and that was help. I was old enough to access the trust fund my grandmother set up for me. I used part of it to establish the Friends Foundation."

She studied Rafe's face, the hard geometry of his jaw. "So now you know everything about me."

"What I know is, I owe my freedom to you."

"I got Nina to the doctor. *He* helped her remember she'd been molested by her stepfather, not raped by you."

"If she'd ended it all, she never would have made it to the doctor," Rafe countered, his voice thick with the emotion she saw in his eyes. "And I'd still be in that cell."

When she pressed her hand against his cheek, she felt the muscles in his jaw clench tight. "I'm so very glad you're not."

Rafe gathered her hand in his. Nothing she could have told him could have jolted him more. He had no clue how to deal with the emotions flooding through him, which made him feel unsteadier. So he did the only thing he could—pushed them aside. For now.

"I expect we're both talked out." He lifted their joined hands and pressed a kiss on the inside of her wrist. Against his mouth, he felt her pulse kick into high speed. "How about we don't talk?"

"You have something else in mind?"

"Yeah." He curled his free hand around the nape of her neck and tugged her closer while need for her crept into his bloodstream to stagger his heart. Lowering his head, he met her lips with his, let the kiss spin out until he was rock-hard and aching.

Her body shifted fluidly, her hands sliding up his bare

chest to link at the nape of his neck. A purr sounded in her throat. "Want to take this into the bedroom?"

"Dammit," he muttered as the practical side of him pinged a warning in his brain. "Dammit," he repeated, and rested his forehead against hers.

"Is this your way of telling me you don't want to go inside?"

He eased his head back. Her hair was mussed, her lips ripe and desire glimmered in her eyes. There was only one thing stopping him.

"I'm out of condoms." It took a concerted effort to keep a groan out of his voice. "Do you by chance have some stored in your nightstand?"

"No." She closed her eyes, eased out a frustrated breath. "Does it help to know I have this weird cycle so I'm on the pill?"

He was tempted, so very tempted to sweep her up and carry her into the bedroom. But the rules he'd established for himself, the control he'd honed over the last five years didn't allow for slipups. Not to a man desperate to call the shots when it came to the direction his life took.

He stroked his palm down her hair. "We have two choices. One, I can hop in the car and go to that upscale convenience store at the entrance to your neighborhood."

She twisted her mouth. "That will take ten minutes. Fifteen, maybe."

"Option two." He slid a hand beneath the white shirt and felt her shudder when his palm cupped her breast. "There's more than one way to derive pleasure." He dipped his head, nuzzled her throat. "Your choice."

"Let's see what's behind door number two," she said, then clamped her mouth on his.

* * *

For a man who had once believed he was dead inside, Rafe suddenly found himself dealing with a complex tangle of emotions. *Trying* to deal with them, he amended while using the back of his hand to swipe sweat and construction dust off his forehead. Problem was, excesses of emotion were not his forte, so he had no clue where to begin the untangling.

All he knew for sure was that Allie had disturbed the efficient peace he'd established in his life and he didn't know what the hell to do about it. Didn't know what he wanted to do.

Frowning, he positioned the tip of a drill bit in the center of the X he'd marked on the wall. He was a man who kept his promises and he'd decided today was as good as any to put in his volunteer labor at the small fixer-upper house owned by the Friends Foundation.

He'd held out a simple and steady hope that by immersing himself in sawdust-filled air and the whine of power tools he could get a handle on what was going on inside of him.

So far he'd installed four doorknobs, three towel rods and was in the process of hanging a medicine cabinet. He had yet to get anything figured out emotion-wise. That did not bode well because he had planned to have things figured out before he dropped by Allie's shop to give her a report on Dena, the abused woman who'd called the foundation's hotline.

His jaw tightened with the knowledge that if it were any other client, he would deliver his report over the phone. But, dammit, he wanted to see Allie. Touch her. *Smell* her.

And if it weren't so freaking hot inside the small bathroom, his brain might kick in and start unraveling his problems. But the heat and air contractor wasn't scheduled to show up until the following day, so Rafe figured he was out of luck.

The drill sent a low-pitched grinding noise through the steamy air as the bit ate into the Sheetrock. He pulled his measuring tape out of his tool belt, rechecked the distance he'd marked from the hole to the second X he'd penciled on the wall. The tape rewound with a snap just as his cell phone rang.

He pulled it off his tool belt, checked the display. Seeing Hank Bishop's name had Rafe's shoulders going stiff. He had followed up all leads on Mercedes McKenzie's murder and gotten nowhere. Junior's claim that he'd been with a woman that night had checked out. Ellen Bishop was still a big question mark, though. As was Joseph Slater, the man who'd lured Allie to her warehouse and tried to turn *him* into roadkill. If something didn't shake loose soon, Rafe was certain his client would do time for killing his mistress.

"Diaz," he answered, and leaned a hip against the sink.

"When I saw you at the vacant building, you told me to try to think about anything Mercedes might have done that was out of the ordinary," Hank Bishop said. "Something that didn't jibe."

"You've thought of something?"

"I don't know if it's important or not, but a couple of weeks before the murder, I was at the condo with Mercedes. I got a call on my cell from a man who said he was interested in investing in the property in the Automobile Alley district that my company was working up a deal to purchase, then turn into condos and retail."

"What specific property is that?"

"That's just it—Guy and I aren't looking to buy any

property in Automobile Alley. I told the caller he'd gotten bad information. I hung up, then went to take a shower. When I got out, I opened the bathroom door to let the steamy air out, and caught a glimpse of Mercedes. She was sitting on the bed, scrolling through information on my cell. When she sensed my watching her, she tossed the phone aside, said it had rung, but the call had gone to voice mail before she could answer. That was strange to begin with, because she'd never answered my phone before."

"Who called?"

"No one," Bishop answered. "When I checked the phone later, no call had come in after the one from the investor with the bad information about the Automobile Alley property. It may mean nothing, but there must be some reason Mercedes lied when I caught her looking at the info in my cell."

"Has to be," Rafe agreed. "Just like there's a reason she had recording equipment installed throughout the condo without ever telling you. We just haven't uncovered those reasons yet."

"I'm nervous, Diaz. If you don't find out who killed Mercedes, I'm going to wind up on trial for her murder."

"I'm working on it," Rafe said. "I've got the copies your secretary made of your cell-phone bills at my office. If you can give me the date and approximate time the call came in, I'll track down the potential investor. See where that leads."

"Hold on while I look at my calendar," Bishop said.

Rafe used his forearm to make another swipe at his sweaty forehead. He hoped to hell this led to something. If not, he'd be giving Hank Bishop tips on how to survive in prison.

Allie stopped dead in her tracks the instant she spotted Rafe through the bathroom's open door. The fact he was talking on his cell phone wasn't the reason she didn't make her presence known.

The sight of him wearing only worn jeans and a tool belt riding gunslinger low on his narrow hips was a prime example of raw male power. Standing there, she felt herself melting like butter in the heat.

Oh, God.

She didn't have to guess how that broad, gleaming-with-sweat chest would feel beneath her hand, her cheek or her mouth. She remembered. Vividly.

She didn't need to speculate about how it would feel if he slid that tough, honed body over hers, either. She remembered that vividly, too.

She didn't need to wonder about the taste and texture of his mouth. She knew. Lord, did she know. Just looking at him turned her blood to steam. She'd never had such a visceral reaction to a man before.

Never been this close to falling in love.

If the sight of him hadn't already brought her up short, that last random thought would have done it.

Oh, no. No. No. *No*. She had no clue where that had come from, but it was crazy. She was *not* falling into anything, much less love. Love made you stupid, vulnerable and unhappy.

Just then, Rafe ended his call and glanced into the bedroom. His gaze slid down her black tank top, dropped to her denim shorts, then slicked down her bare legs to her tennis shoes. It was as if his eyes touched every part of her with a hot, feral look. Then his gaze rose slowly and locked with hers. The heat that settled in his eyes made her clothes feel too tight.

His mouth curved slightly at the sides. "I didn't know you'd be here."

"Same goes for you."

"We had a deal." He rested his hands at his hips. "I gave you my word I'd put in some time here if you got me into the silent auction. I always keep my word."

Which was just one of the things about him that drew her. As did his quiet strength. His tenacity. Even his aloneness called to something deep inside her soul. She was fascinated by his intelligence and discipline.

At that instant, her throat snapped shut. She fought to catch her breath. Her heart hammered.

And her hands trembled.

This was the moment, she realized. The moment that the bottom dropped away and sent her crashing, headfirst into love.

He inclined his head toward the sink. "I'm about ready to hang the medicine cabinet, but I need an extra hand. You available?"

"Sure," she answered, keeping her voice as casual as his.

She walked toward him, feeling as if she'd just stepped onto a tightwire strung between two very high cliffs.

She just hoped there was a net somewhere to catch her if she fell.

Chapter 12

"Hold it steady while I get my side secured on the hanger," Rafe said.

"Will do." Gripping the opposite end of the medicine cabinet, Allie willed her heart rate to steady, which was wasted effort because only two inches separated her from bulging biceps and muscles rippling beneath tight olive skin.

Oh, my.

"So what brings you here today?" he asked, keeping his attention focused on his task.

She scrambled to think past the sudden discovery that male sweat could, indeed, be an aphrodisiac.

"It wasn't on my schedule. But I found out the mom and her kids who are going to live here are coming by later to see the house for the first time. Before they get here, I want to touch up a few places where the wall paint went on too thin."

"I planned to drop by your shop." Rafe tested his side of the cabinet, then moved to hers. "To update you on Dena."

Allie's nerves went on point. Like an invisible splinter beneath her skin, thoughts of the woman and her young son had worried her since the call came to the hotline.

"Can you update me and work at the same time?"

Rafe sent her a sardonic look. "I think I can manage."

The bathroom was so small she had no space to shift away when he reached for her side of the cabinet. When his arms brushed across hers, she swallowed hard. "Okay, Mr. I-Can-Talk-and-Chew-Gum-at-the-Same-Time, tell me."

"Dena's last name is Anderson. Her common-law husband is Eric Postelle. He's got a rap sheet, mostly for arrests that involve alcohol. Public drunk. One DUI. The latest arrest was for assault. Postelle got wasted in a bar—there's the alcohol—and hit the bartender over the head with a pool cue."

"Nice guy."

"The bartender didn't think so. Postelle did time and he's out on parole."

"Can anything be done to keep him away from Dena and their son?"

"Already taken care of." Rafe snaked his hand behind the edge of the cabinet, slid its hanger onto the hook. "That'll hold it."

Allie laid a hand on his arm when he started gathering his tools. "What do you mean 'already taken care of'?"

Rafe shifted to face her. With her nose so close to his bare chest, she could smell the work of the day on him, the faint tang of healthy sweat, the traces of Sheetrock dust.

"It stands to reason someone with that many alcohol-related arrests isn't likely to stay away from a bar. Just stepping inside one is an automatic violation of his parole."

As he talked, Rafe picked up a tape measure off the vanity, stuck it in his tool belt. "I staked out the house where Dena and Postelle live, so I was there when he got home from the fishing trip. He stayed long enough to change clothes, then drove off. I followed him to a bar. He ordered a pitcher of beer and played a game of pool. The first time he bent over to make a shot, I saw a gun tucked into the back waistband of his jeans. I called 911 from a pay phone. Said I was a concerned citizen who didn't want to give my name and wanted to report that I'd just seen an armed felon in a bar. It didn't take long for a couple of black and whites to arrive. Or for the cops to escort Postelle outside wearing cuffs."

"Is it for sure he'll go back to prison?"

"If getting caught inside the bar doesn't totally violate his parole, the weapon does. He'll be locked up for another year at least." Rafe's forehead furrowed. "Having been there myself, sending people to prison isn't high on my list. But I have no problem doing it to a drunk who beats a woman and has his own kid in his sights to receive poundings, too."

Relief coursed through Allie. "Hopefully Dena will call the hotline again so we can help her plan for the future."

"Because of you, there's a happy ending."

"And you. Thank you, Rafe."

He gazed down at her. "All in a day's work."

"Just like your being here is. You promised to put in some volunteer time and that's what you're doing."

"I'm a man of my word."

"What you are is a good man. A caring man." She

cupped her palm against his cheek. "That makes you special." He was everything she'd never known she wanted. Everything she'd never allowed herself to dream about on long solitary nights in her bed when half-formed thoughts surfaced from her subconscious.

She hadn't expected to fall in love, but the feeling was there, big and bold and beautiful. It was impossible to turn away from those feelings, even if she'd wanted to. For the first time in her life, she was following her heart, allowing it to lead her even though her head told her she might regret it. For now, though, she was going to give their relationship a chance.

He tugged her hand away from his cheek and pressed a kiss against the center of her palm. "Sounds like you're trying to slip a halo over my head. I did what you hired me to do."

The gesture made her heart flutter. Wanting to give back as good as she got, she ran her fingertips over the crisp black hairs on his chest and deliberately dropped her voice to a low, seductive purr. "This brings me to a question about your fee."

A thrill of dark pleasure rippled through her body at the lethal spark in his eyes. "We didn't discuss my fee."

"Exactly." She hip-swayed a step closer. "Are you planning on giving me an invoice? Or would you like to take your fee out in trade?"

"Let me think about that."

It wasn't just her touch or the sexy rasp in her voice that heated Rafe's blood. She'd clipped her golden hair back and, thanks to the heat and humidity, small, damp tendrils had escaped around her ears and clung to her nape. Why that made him even hotter, he couldn't say. It just did.

One-handed, he unbuckled his tool belt and dropped it

to the floor while he snagged her wrist and jerked her against him.

"I'm done thinking." When he crushed his mouth to hers, all the uncertainty, the rolling emotions he'd been struggling against faded at the first hot taste of her. *Need.* The word hammered in his brain. He'd never needed anyone more than he needed her at this moment.

And then he felt it, something inside him slipped off the chain, something feral and prowling, something totally out of his control. He could smell it, smell the hunger in her, the craving. It was as strong as his, as basic and primitive as his.

With the toe of one boot, he kicked the bathroom door shut, then whirled her back against it.

Her breath caught as she gripped his shoulders. "Does this mean you decided to take your fee out in—"

He cut her off with a kiss that was even wilder than the first. Hungrier. Deeper. He lifted her onto her toes and pressed in hard against her, grinding his erection into the softness of her mound. With a small moan at the back of her throat, she wrapped her arms around him.

She was pure energy in his arms, snapping and pulsing to life with a greed that staggered him. She had one hand tangled in his hair, holding his head still while she kissed him back, her teeth and tongue voracious, one hand clawing at his shoulder. Starving, he dived deeper into her mouth while her heart hammered against his.

On an oath, he unsnapped her shorts, dragged down the zipper, then thrust his hand inside her panties and curled his fingers up into her while his palm rode her. She bucked under the lash of abrupt desire, growing wet around his fingers, clenching them with her body.

His system on fire for her, he shucked her out of her

shorts and panties. He freed himself, then, gripping her hips, plunged into her where they stood.

He could hear her quick, breathy murmurs but didn't know what she was asking. Didn't care. She locked herself around him, let him drive her ruthlessly, crest after torrential crest. And met him thrust for greedy, desperate thrust.

He felt her body shudder, then go limp. His fingers tightening on her hips, he pumped into her until he went over the edge.

He slapped his hands against the wall to keep his balance, struggled to ease his breathing, clear his fevered brain.

It cleared slowly, with crystal clarity.

"Hell."

"More like heaven," she murmured, her voice breathy and raw.

There was no point in apologies, he thought. They'd both wanted fast and urgent. More like *craved* it.

So much that he'd totally lost control. Hadn't used a condom. Hadn't even *thought* about one.

That knowledge put a knot in his gut as her legs slid down his and she braced her back against the wall. He stepped away, neatened himself with brisk movements, then zipped up his jeans.

Her hips made a sexy little shimmy when she pulled up her panties and shorts. The movement had him gritting his teeth.

He had never intended to allow anyone to have that kind of power over him and the fact that she did terrified him. How the hell had it gotten to the point where everything about her threatened to swallow him?

He needed time. Time to step back, gain some distance. He'd let things move too fast, to get out of control. He intended to fix that by putting the wheel firmly back in his own hands.

"I was rough. Did I hurt you?"

The hard edge in his voice had Allie's brows drawing together. But it was the grim look in his eyes that sent nerves moving into her stomach. "You didn't hurt me. And I was as rough with you as you were with me."

"There's something I didn't get around to. I should have. There's no excuse."

She understood what he meant. "I told you the other night that I'm on the pill."

"Dammit, that doesn't matter." He stabbed his fingers through his dark hair. "What matters is that I didn't even *think* about using a condom."

"Neither did I." Her mouth, still on fire from his, curved. "We both got carried away."

"That might be something you're willing to shrug off, but I'm not. I lost control."

"We both did." Something's wrong was all she could think as she gazed up at him. *Very wrong.* "We can agree not to get carried away again without protection."

"Dammit, I don't lose control. I *never* lose control." His hands curled into fists. "Except with you."

Twin demons of hurt and temper stabbed at her heart. "This isn't really about a condom, is it, Rafe? It sounds more like your problem is, you don't want to want me."

"What I don't want is to lose control of any portion of my life. I did that once and paid a high price. I don't intend to let anyone have that kind of power over me again."

His biting tone had her temper spiking. "I wasn't aware I did."

He jerked his tool belt off the floor, then stepped toward the door. "I've got to get to my office to check some phone records."

"Don't let me keep you." So he wouldn't see that her hands had begun to shake, she curled her fingers into her palms. "The last thing *I* intend to do is spend time with a man who is disgusted by the fact that he wants me."

"Disgusted?" His hand stopped in midair as he reached for the doorknob. "That's not what I said. Dammit, I didn't *say* that."

"Mince words all you want, but that was your meaning. You want me and that upsets you." She checked her watch. "I need to get the painting done so I can get back to my shop."

He jerked the door open, stepped out of the bathroom, then paused. He closed his eyes. A muscle ticked in his jaw. When he turned back to face her, his eyes were bleak. "Look, I just need to get some things straight in my head."

She stepped to the door, shut it in his face and turned the lock with a hard, audible click.

She leaned back against the door, her breath shallow. If she needed a reminder why she'd sworn off relationships, this was it. In the end, someone walked away. And someone got left behind. In shreds.

Growing up, she'd vowed to never care enough about anyone that their leaving would matter. That she'd broken that vow willingly didn't lessen the ache Rafe's words had settled inside her.

It sure as hell hadn't taken long for her joyous bubble of being in love to burst.

Her lips trembled, but she firmed them against a sob. Just the idea of standing there, blubbering over a man scraped at her pride. She had her work and her friends—that was enough. It had always been enough.

She would make sure it was enough.

Even as she squared her shoulders, she admitted she would never be the same. Because she knew, she just knew, that Rafe Diaz was the only man who would ever find his way into her heart.

She had a terrible feeling it was going to be hell getting him out.

Hours later, Rafe sat at the desk in his office, waiting for a phone call while the facts he hadn't wanted to face before now pounded him on his chest and shook him by the collar. He had panicked, that was all there was to it. Panicked because his not even thinking about using a condom drove home the truth he'd been avoiding. He'd been content with the emotionally sterile existence he'd designed for himself until he'd walked into Allie's shop to interview her. From that moment his life had felt like a runaway train.

Despite his best intentions not to let her matter, she did. She had made him long for something more, made him forget the controls he'd carefully put in place that had kept his feelings locked inside of him. Today in that bathroom, the helplessness of his need for her had swamped him. Made him panic so that he'd pushed her away. *Hurt her.*

When what he should have done was held her close and told her he was in love with her.

There. It was out, something he hadn't wanted to admit but couldn't escape. He was in love with her.

The realization sent emotions rushing into his throat. And his heart. Myriad, indefinable emotions that expanded to fill all those dark, empty places inside him.

When he'd fallen, he had no clue. He just knew he had.

Hard. And now, because he was an idiot, he'd be lucky if she ever spoke to him again.

He glanced around his neat-as-a-pin office that was squeezed into the top floor of a narrow downtown building. For the first time, the controlled efficient business environment he'd created felt barren. Cold. Which was what his life would go back to being without Allie in it: nothing around him. Nothing on the horizon. All alone.

No highs. No lows.

His feeling dead on the inside and thinking that was how he wanted to live the rest of his life. It wasn't. The solitude he'd once felt content in now merely looked like a long stretch of lonely.

Elbows propped on the desk, he dropped his face into his hands. Somehow, someway, he was going to have to make things right again.

When the telephone rang, he checked caller ID. And eased out a relieved breath that Quinn Underwood had returned his call.

Maybe, just maybe, the man had information that would break open the Bishop case. And give him something else to think about besides Allie Fielding.

Rafe answered and introduced himself. Then said, "I understand you called Hank Bishop to ask questions about some property in the Automobile Alley area."

"That's right." Underwood's sandpaper voice sounded like the irreversible result of three packs a day. "Bishop said he didn't know what property I was talking about, then hung up. Not exactly a good way to go about racking up potential investors."

"According to Mr. Bishop, his company wasn't looking to purchase property in that part of town."

"Well, that's not what Bishop's partner told me and a few others."

Rafe frowned. "Guy Jones told you they were looking to invest in Automobile Alley property?"

"Damn right. He gave me the impression he was speaking for both himself and Bishop. I've known Guy for a few years, but I've never met his brother-in-law. I don't invest money with people I haven't dealt with face-to-face. That's why I called Bishop, to set up a meeting."

Rafe dropped his gaze to the set of records for the cell phone that Hank Bishop had supplied to his mistress. "You also got a call from Mercedes McKenzie. That would have been a couple of hours after you phoned Hank Bishop."

"I got a call from a woman saying she was Bishop's admin assistant. I don't remember her name."

"Why did she call you?"

"To find out what I knew about the Automobile Alley property. She said Bishop wanted her to check on some facts."

Rafe narrowed his eyes. "So you told her what you knew?"

"I did. Which was damn strange. If his partner was putting the deal together, why the hell didn't Bishop just ask Guy Jones?"

"Good question," Rafe agreed. "Did you invest in the property?"

"Hell no," Underwood answered, his smoker's rasp grating across the line. "It sounded to me like no one in that company knew what the others were doing. I called Jones, told him what had happened and that I wasn't impressed. I advised him not to expect money from me."

Rafe thanked the man, then hung up. He thought back to the day he'd met Bishop at the vacant building that Guy

Jones had wanted their company to buy. When Bishop refused, Jones's temper had flared.

The wheels in Rafe's head turned with possibilities, but there was one fact he needed to check with his client. However, instead of dialing Bishop's cell phone, he called his client's office so his secretary would answer. After she told him Guy Jones had called in sick that morning, she transferred the call to her boss's line. Hank Bishop answered on the first ring.

"Do you have a female admin assistant?" Rafe asked.

"Yes."

"Would she have had any reason to call a potential investor about information on property in Automobile Alley?"

"She doesn't get into specific stuff like that with clients. Why, what have you found out?"

Rafe held back from mentioning he suspected Guy Jones might have been wheeling and dealing behind his partner's back. Bishop was out on bond for murder—if he confronted his brother-in-law and things got heated enough that the cops were called, Bishop's bail would be revoked and he'd spend the time between now and his trial behind bars.

"I need to check a few more facts before I lay things out for you," Rafe answered.

Bishop eased out a frustrated breath. "Diaz, I hope to hell whatever those facts are gets me off the hook for Mercedes's murder."

"I'll do my best to make that happen," Rafe said. He ended the call and tugged the phone book out of his desk drawer.

Because Guy Jones had called in sick to work that morning, Rafe flipped to the page that showed the man's home address.

* * *

By the time Rafe located Guy Jones's sprawling three-story house, long fingers of late-afternoon shadows had spread across the manicured lawn. He spotted Jones's daughter heading across the front porch toward the driveway where a sporty little powder-blue MG sat. Dressed in a sleeveless yellow top and white capris, Katie Jones looked pencil-thin. To Rafe's investigator's eye, the young woman had dropped a few pounds since the silent auction.

He caught up with her in the driveway just as she reached the driver's side of the MG.

"Miss Jones? I'm Rafe Diaz. We met at the silent auction."

"You're the PI my Uncle Hank hired, right?" she asked, peering at him through enormous black sunglasses. Her dark hair was pulled back in such a tight bun that the bones in her face looked as if they'd been sharpened on a whetstone.

"Yes. Something's come up that I need to speak to your father about. I understand he called in sick today."

"He had some sort of stomach thing this morning, but he's okay now. He left to run a couple of errands." She pointed at the house with her chin. "My mom's home if you want to leave a message for him. Or you can call his cell."

"I need to see him in person. Do you know where he went?"

"The only place I'm sure of is that he's going by Silk & Secrets to drop off a check to pay for my trousseau." Her mouth curved. "I go in tomorrow for my final fitting and I want to bring home all the accessories. They have to be paid for so I can do that."

While she talked, Katie dug into the oversized purse slung over one shoulder and pulled out car keys and an iPod. "Actually, I think my wedding's the reason my dad all of a sudden has stomach problems."

"How so?"

"Money. I'm not good about sticking to a budget." She shrugged. "He turned as white as a sheet a while ago when I told him I'd added a purse to the accessories I'm getting from Allie."

"A purse," Rafe repeated, his mind clicking to the fact that Mercedes McKenzie's killer had dumped the contents of her purse on the floor of her bedroom. "If it's shaped like a clamshell, I saw it the other day when I was at Allie's warehouse."

Katie's face brightened. "That's the one. I *know* it was designed by Uncle Hank's mistress and that my Aunt Ellen will freak if she sees me with it, but it matches my going-away outfit. I just had to have it."

Rafe narrowed his eyes, remembering. The silent auction. Guy Jones looking surprised when told the jeweled purse his sister-in-law had lobbed at Allie had been designed by Mercedes McKenzie. Purses that Allie sold in her shop.

Hours later, Silk & Secrets was burglarized. All clothing had been thrown on the floor. Every purse had been pulled out of the display case, opened and tossed aside. Opened, as if the burglar had been searching for something in one of the purses.

Presumably, whatever that something was hadn't been found because Joseph Slater later lured Allie to her warehouse, where the purses were made.

Rafe stabbed his fingers into the back pockets of his jeans. Jones's involvement in a real estate scheme he'd concealed from his partner, combined with his surprised look when he discovered Allie sold a line of McKenzie purses in her shop had the hairs on the back of Rafe's neck standing on end.

And that wasn't all. Jones had lied about hanging around to help his wife calm down their drunken sister-in-law whom they'd driven home from the auction. It was possible he had used that time to arrange for Joseph Slater to burglarize Silk & Secrets. Dread splashed through Rafe's heart like acid.

"How long has your dad been gone?"

Katie lifted an impossibly thin shoulder. "Twenty, thirty minutes. I told him he'd better hurry if he was going to get to Allie's shop before it closed."

Rafe wheeled around, dashed for his car.

Chapter 13

She needed girl-talk, Allie decided while snipping a stray thread off the ivory satin basque Katie Jones was scheduled to try on in the morning. The clock on the long-legged design table tucked into a corner of Silk & Secret's plush fitting room showed it was one minute to closing time. Claire would be at her antique shop next door and Liz was due off her shift in an hour.

Allie had stocked the shop's small kitchen area with several bottles of good wine. Dinner could be ordered in. And it was a sure bet Claire had a quart of the chocolate cherry ice cream she kept on hand in case of girlfriend emergencies.

Allie figured the ache in her heart qualified as one.

She closed her eyes on a wave of pain. Dammit, hours had passed since the melt-your-skin-off-your-bones encounter with Rafe, but she could still feel the imprint of his mouth, his hands on her. She could still *taste* him.

"Not for long," she muttered. She might not be able to do anything about the bruising her heart had taken, but she'd do her best to erase his taste. A combination of wine and ice cream ought to do the trick. At least she hoped it would.

She replaced the scissors on her design table. After diverting around the pinning platform that faced a soaring trifold antique mirror, she draped the basque on the powder-pink love seat beside the other pieces of Katie's wedding lingerie.

Allie was on her way to lock the shop's front door when she glimpsed a tall, brawny man rushing across Reunion Square. When he came abreast of the front window, she realized it was Guy Jones.

Although she was in no mood to deal with a last-minute customer, Allie forced her mouth to curve. Guy and his wife had spent a hefty sum on their daughter's wedding trousseau and they deserved the best service Allie could offer.

"Hello, Guy, how are you?"

"Fine." He was wearing pleated khaki slacks with what appeared to be permanent ironed-in wrinkles, a striped short-sleeved dress shirt, black loafers with dusty toes and a watch large enough to be a cell phone. "I stopped by to give you a check for Katie's stuff."

"I appreciate that." Allie stepped behind the glass counter to one side of the door. "Although Katie could have brought it when she comes in tomorrow to try on her trousseau."

Guy dug out his wallet, pulled out a check and handed it across the counter. "I brought it by because I want to take a look at the stuff."

Allie glanced up from the receipt drawer. "You want to see Katie's complete trousseau?"

"Yeah." He wiped a palm over his dark, thinning hair. "My

wife's seen everything, but I don't have a clue what all Katie's picked out. I like to know what I'm getting for my money."

"Of course." Allie closed the drawer. It was the first time she'd had a father of the bride make that sort of request—and truth be told, it seemed a little odd—but Guy was footing the bill, so she would accommodate him.

Wine and ice cream, she thought, would have to wait.

"Because Katie will be here in the morning, I've got everything laid out for her to try on. Just follow me."

When they stepped into the fitting room, Allie gestured toward the love seat. "Katie's bridal lingerie is there. Her gowns and robes are hanging here." Allie indicated the antique coat tree that held numerous padded hangers dripping with a rainbow of silky garments. "Other items—"

"She mentioned a purse." Guy's gaze swept the room. "Said she had to have it because it matches some outfit."

Allie arched a brow at the sudden briskness in his tone. "The clamshell." Diverting around the pinning platform, she stepped to the design table and lifted the lid off a hot pink box with Silk & Secrets scrawled in italics across its top.

"This will look gorgeous with Katie's going-away outfit," Allie said while retrieving the beaded bag from its tissue-paper nest.

"The McKenzie woman designed it, right?"

"Yes." She saw Guy's eyes sharpen when she handed him the purse. She wondered if his reaction was due to the fact his brother-in-law had been involved with Mercedes and had been arrested for her murder.

Guy opened the purse, jabbed his beefy fingers inside and groped at the lining.

Allie had to hold back from cautioning him to be careful.

While she watched, a mix of emotions washed over his face that Allie was at a loss to read.

He snapped the purse shut. "I'm taking this with me."

She furrowed her forehead. "Katie is bringing her going-away outfit in tomorrow to try on with its lingerie and accessories. The clamshell goes with that outfit. It would be more convenient if you left it here."

His eyes went hard and flat. "Did you forget about the check I just gave you?" Guy's voice had lost all casualness and Allie noted that a fine sheen of sweat now covered his upper lip. "I can haul all of Katie's stuff out of here now if I want."

"You can." Allie's stomach quivered at the sudden change in his demeanor. "I merely wanted to point out that it would be inconvenient—"

The aggressive step he took toward her sent her two swift steps backward. Her hip rammed into one corner of the design table, making her wince while alarm bells shrilled in her head. Something was terribly wrong.

"Things have been *inconvenient* for me, too," he snapped, his eyes gleaming with sudden fury. His chest heaved as if his breathing had suddenly become labored and his voice had turned hoarse. It was as if the man had begun unraveling in front of her. "Just give me the box the damn purse goes in."

"Of course." The nerves jumping in her stomach echoed in Allie's voice. He stood so close she could smell the sourness of his sweat through the faint wisps of lavender that scented the shop's air. She had no idea what was going on and she didn't care—she intended to put as much distance between herself and Guy Jones as possible. But her hip was wedged against the table, making it impossible to inch away in any direction.

She forced her mouth to curve, her posture to remain relaxed. "I apologize, Guy. Usually it's the bride and her mother whose nerves fray over wedding details." As she spoke, Allie angled sideways. With her body blocking his view, she groped her hand up the side of the table until her trembling fingers connected with the cold steel of her scissors. "It's easy to forget that fathers of the bride are also susceptible to getting the jitters."

"Yeah, jitters," Guy agreed. "I've got them, all right."

"Looks that way."

With the scissors gripped in her hand, Allie whipped her head toward the arched entrance in time to see Rafe step into the dressing room. Earlier, he'd been the last man she wanted to see. Now faced with Guy Jones's erratic behavior, she was grateful for Rafe's presence.

She heard Guy's breath hiss out. "What are you doing here, Diaz?"

"Looking for you," Rafe said levelly. Fingers jammed into the back pockets of his jeans, he strolled to the center of the room. "I dropped by your house. Your daughter told me I could probably catch up with you here."

Guy stood close enough to Allie that she felt him stiffen. "Why are you looking for me?"

The words came out on a low growl, ramping up the volume on the warning bells already going off inside Allie's head. She could almost smell Guy's tension, his fear, and suspicion chilled her body. Had Rafe found something that connected the man to Mercedes's murder?

Rafe set his jaw. Jones's stiff demeanor, the wariness in his eyes convinced Rafe that the man had killed McKenzie. But knowing it and proving it were different matters. He needed Jones to confess. But his first priority was getting the man away from Allie. So Rafe kept his voice calm, steady, as he responded to Guy's question. "I need to talk to you about your brother-in-law's case."

"What about it?"

Rafe flicked his gaze toward Allie. Her face was flushed, her mouth set. "I'd prefer not to discuss this in front of Miss Fielding." Rafe tipped his head toward her. "No offense."

"None taken." The nerves rolling in Allie's stomach made her voice sound like rusted metal. Her fingers felt numb against the cold steel of the scissors.

Rafe made his slow way around the pinning platform. "Jones, how about you and I walk over to the bar on the other side of the square? We can have a drink while we chat. On me."

"I'd rather talk here." Guy jerked his head toward Allie. "With her staying right where she is."

Sick panic clawed inside Allie. Rafe clearly wanted to get Guy out of the shop. That he insisted on staying—with her beside him—made her feel like a hostage. The adrenaline rushing through her blood pushed at her to bolt. To run. Yet, all of her instincts told her to take her cues from the PI watching her with those dark, steady eyes.

"Your call." Rafe took an idle step closer. "The bottom line is, every lead I check on this case points back to Hank. It's looking like he killed Mercedes McKenzie."

Allie's breathing shallowed. She knew that wasn't true—he'd told her he was convinced Hank Bishop was innocent. She felt awareness creep under her skin. She was certain now that Rafe had found evidence linking Guy to the murder. That would explain the man's erratic behavior. And the reason Rafe was trying so hard to get him out of the shop. *Away from her.*

"Have you told Hank?" Guy asked. A muscle ticked in his jaw while a bead of sweat trickled down the side of his face. His chest heaved in and out and Allie could hear the quickening in his breathing.

"Not yet." Rafe paused beside the antique coat tree, ran a fingertip down the sleeve of a peach-colored robe. "It'd be best to have a family member with me when I do. For support. Because Hank's son is ticked off at him and Ellen has filed for divorce, you're it."

Allie scrolled her gaze downward. Guy had such a tight hold on the clamshell purse that his knuckles showed white beneath his skin. In hindsight, she realized his sole reason for coming to the shop today was to retrieve the purse. Somehow, someway, it must be connected to the murder.

At that point she didn't care how. The situation was so volatile that the very air crackled with electricity. Guy's stress level seemed to inch up with each passing minute. If he *had* killed Mercedes, there was no telling what he might do if he felt cornered. Rafe wanted to get Guy out of the shop. So did she. She could try to help make that happen.

"He's right, Guy," she said, forcing her voice to remain level while her fingers trembled against the scissors. "No matter what Hank has done, he needs his family's support. Go with Rafe."

As if he'd suddenly realized how close Rafe now stood, Guy shifted a step sideways and bumped into Allie. "I've got other stuff to do right now. You go on, Diaz. I'll drop by Hank's later."

Rafe's eyes narrowed, glinted. "Sorry, that plan doesn't work for me."

"Bastard!" Guy shouted, fury resonating in the curse. He swivelled, his lips curled back. Before Allie could think, before she could react, he'd whipped an arm around her throat. Her lungs heaved as he jerked her back against his chest.

"You listen to me, Diaz. I'm not going to the chair for Mercedes's murder! She was blackmailing me. She was vicious. Greedy. She asked for it."

"I know." Rafe kept his gaze locked with Jones's. He couldn't—*wouldn't*—let himself think about the damage the bastard's beefy arm could do to Allie's throat.

"You know?" Against her spine, Allie felt the words shudder inside Jones. "You know what Mercedes did?"

"Most of it," Rafe answered. "You were working a deal under the radar to buy property in Automobile Alley. You didn't want Hank to know about it. But Mercedes found out and threatened to tell him." The theories Rafe had already formulated in his head clicked neatly into place. "What did she do? Call and invite you to her condo?"

"That's right." Jones's voice was a hard rasp in Allie's right ear. "Hank had kept their affair secret so I had no idea she was involved with him. She said one of the investors I was working with referred her and she wanted to get in on the deal. She sounded legit. I went to her place. Laid out everything. She said she'd be in touch."

Rafe eased an inch closer. "And when she got back to you, she told you she'd recorded your conversation, using all that high-tech equipment hidden in the condo. She threatened to tell Hank if you didn't pay, right?"

"Two million!" Guy shouted. "I'd barely been able to scrape up that amount for the deposit on the property."

"Which you would lose if the deal fell through." Rafe looked at the thick arm clenched around Allie's throat. At the scissors she held gripped against her thigh. One false move on anyone's part and she might die. The knots in his stomach tightened. "The deal would fall through, wouldn't it, if Hank found out?"

"He was fed up with me! Kept telling me I needed to hold up my end, bring in some profits. Think outside some damn box. I knew he was getting ready to dissolve the partnership. For years he'd brought in all the major clients. The profits. If he walked, he'd keep everything that had his fingerprints on it and I'd wind up with nothing."

Rafe nodded slowly. "You were desperate. So you went back to Mercedes's condo."

"Not to kill her. To try to talk her out of going to Hank. The bimbo laughed at me. Said how Hank thought I was pathetic." Guy's voice broke. "I grabbed her throat, squeezed until she told me she'd recorded our conversation on a thumbdrive. Hid it in her purse."

"After she was dead, you went upstairs and dumped out her purse," Rafe added. "It wasn't there."

"Or in any of the other damn purses in her closet."

"You didn't know she designed purses, did you?" Rafe asked. Dammit, he needed an opening. Needed to keep Jones talking until he saw a way to get Allie clear.

"Not until the silent auction. That's when I found out."

"You hired Slater to break in here that same night."

"You shot him!" Jones shouted. "I just needed a damn break. Now it's time to make my own."

When his arm tightened against Allie's windpipe, panic and nausea swirled inside her, rolling up the back of her throat.

"I'm taking her with me." Guy jerked her back one stumbling step.

"I don't think so." Rafe's voice had gone cold. Unemotional.

"Think again, Diaz. You try to stop me, I'll snap her neck."

A jolt of sheer terror made Allie's heart almost freeze in her chest. Tears stung her eyes. He had killed once out of desperation. She had no reason to think Guy would spare her.

"I'm warning you, Diaz." He yanked her back, her feet tripping over his. "Stay where you are or she dies."

Allie tightened her fingers on the scissors. With prayers screaming in her head, she swung her arm, stabbed the tip into Guy's thigh.

He howled. Staggering sideways, he loosened the vicious grip on her throat. Rafe's hand locked on her arm. He tugged her forward. To safety.

Trembling, gasping for air, Allie leaned against her design table. She heard a dull, sickening thud. Her chin came up in time to see Guy land backward across the pinning platform, blood gushing from his nose. Rafe stepped into her line of vision, fury glinting in his dark eyes.

In one smooth move, he grabbed Guy Jones by one shoulder and slammed his fist into his jaw.

For Allie, the following hours passed in a hazy blur of activity. She remembered Rafe carrying her to the love seat, his eyes looking tormented while he checked her neck for injury. Recalled how the cops summoned by his 911 call swarmed into her shop, followed by a stricken Claire, who gripped her hand while an EMT checked the bruises on her throat. Could readily picture Liz in official cop mode, standing across the dressing room, talking to Rafe in quiet tones. And finally riding with Liz to police headquarters for an interview.

That done, Allie had called Claire for a ride home. Wanting nothing more than to be alone with her own thoughts, she assured her friend she was fine and planned to go to bed.

Instead she'd changed into a tank top and shorts, poured a glass of wine and made a beeline for her boathouse's back deck. The pale moon lit the river flowing silently by in subdued shades of gray and black.

She lifted the wineglass off the table beside her chair just as footsteps sounded. When Rafe stepped around the corner of the boathouse into a patch of moonlight, her heart kicked once, hard, and she faltered, the glass partway to her mouth.

"What are you doing here?"

"I needed to see you."

He didn't really *need* anything from her, Allie thought with tears stinging her eyes.

Slowly, she lowered the glass. "Well, it's been an interesting day, all the way around."

"True." Rafe gazed down at the woman he now accepted that he loved. The woman he had stupidly pushed away.

Her skin looked sheet pale in the moonlight. Just as pale as it had been earlier when Jones loomed over her, his arm locked around her delicate throat. That image started Rafe's hands trembling, so he stuffed his fingers into the back pocket of his jeans.

"I wanted to check on you. Had to make sure you're really okay."

Her throat impossibly dry, Allie took a sip of wine before setting the glass on the table. "I'm fine."

"Are you sure?"

Go away. The words were on the tip of her tongue, but

she couldn't say them. Not when she wanted only him. Without the courage to send him away, she gave him a curt nod. "Liz says she thinks the DA will work a deal with Jones."

"Makes sense. He didn't take a weapon with him when he went to Mercedes's condo. Because cause of death was strangulation, a good defense attorney will claim there was no premeditation on Jones's part."

Allie stared out at the dark river. "Liz said they found the thumbdrive hidden under the lining in the clamshell purse. Remember my telling you that Mercedes came to the warehouse hours before she was murdered?"

"I remember. You said Bishop had just told her they were leaving for Paris that night. She was frazzled. Rushed."

Allie grazed a fingertip across the bruises on her throat. "I had the items for Katie Jones's trousseau on one of the worktables. Mercedes asked me who they were for. I told her, even mentioned that there were more items being sewn, but we had two months to go before the wedding."

"That told Mercedes the thumbdrive would be safe in the purse until she got back from Paris," Rafe said. "Could she have slipped it under the lining without anyone seeing?"

"Yes. I had to deal with another matter upstairs. She could have taken the purse then, slit the lining, restitched it, then replaced it on the worktable without anyone noticing."

"When Jones's daughter told him today about that particular purse, he knew it was possible that was where Mercedes had hidden the thumbdrive."

"So he headed for my shop." Allie shoved back a frisson of the danger that still clung to her senses. She was safe now. The terror was over. As was her relationship with Rafe.

She stood, walked to the deck's railing and stared out

at the dark water. "I haven't thanked you yet for helping me get away from Guy. I'm grateful."

It was worse, Rafe realized. That cool, polite tone was worse than a shouted curse.

"You don't have anything to thank me for." He stood, moved to the railing and leaned his back against it so he could see her face. His chest had gone tight. "You did a damn good job with those scissors. Jones will be walking with a limp for a while."

"Either way, it's over. Everything's over." She gripped the wooden railing and looked away. It took too much to look into his eyes. "Thank you for dropping by to check on me."

She was done with him. The thought put a chill in Rafe's blood every bit as sharp as that he'd felt when she'd been in danger. He couldn't lose her. She had to listen to him. She had to understand.

"Allie, I need to explain something to you." His voice was as soft as a whisper on the night air. "I need you to *let* me explain."

"You don't need to tell me what I already know. You want total control over your life, your emotions."

"I thought I did. For a long time, that's what I thought." His hand settled on hers. "I grew up wanting to be a cop. That's all I ever wanted to be. When I got arrested, that dream didn't just fade. It got yanked away and smashed before my eyes."

Allie pulled her bottom lip between her teeth. She wanted to move her hand away from his, but she couldn't make herself do it. His voice was steady, yet raw. As raw as the emotions churning inside of her.

"In prison, I lost the freedom to make choices. The only thing I could regulate was my own emotions. I got good at controlling them. That was the only way to escape where I was. By not allowing myself to react. To feel."

"I understand." He had to leave, she thought. He had to leave now, before she crumbled. She tugged her hand from beneath his, shifted to face him. "It must feel good to have cleared Hank Bishop. I'm sure he'll send more clients your way."

To keep from reaching for her, Rafe curled his fingers into his palms. His throat ached. He couldn't clear it. "Do you think my getting more clients matters?"

"Yes, I do. I think your job, the life you've made for yourself matters a great deal to you."

"I thought it did, too. Just like I thought I had everything figured out. Planned."

It was Rafe's turn to look away. There was ice in his belly—he was terrified he'd already lost her.

"But none of it matters more than you. Since the day I first walked into your shop and saw you again, I've felt like I was sinking in quicksand. I thought if I could just keep things under control, that I would regain my footing. But each time I saw you, I sank a little deeper. Today when we were together, when we made love, I went all the way under: Fast. Hard. And deep. I was terrified."

She blinked. "Terrified?"

"That I no longer had power over anything. My life. My emotions. It felt like I'd been tossed back in prison. I panicked. I hurt you by making you think I didn't want to want you. What I don't want is that life I had so carefully orchestrated because you're not a part of it. The only life I want is one with you in it."

He stepped toward her, skimmed a fingertip along her jaw. "I'm sorry I hurt you. Sorry I walked out." His palm cupped her cheek. "If you tell me to go, I will. But I'll be back. I love you, Allie."

"You—" She had to take a step back, had to press a hand to her heart. "You love me."

"You don't have a lot of faith in relationships. Considering what you saw while growing up, I don't blame you. But I'm asking you to give ours another try. I think together we can beat the odds."

Her head was still spinning. He loved her. The pressure in Allie's chest all but burst her heart. "Rafe..."

Could she do it? Open her heart to him again? Take the scariest chance of her life?

He moved in, gathered her to him. "Please don't tell me it's too late. That I've ruined things between us."

She looked into his dark eyes and saw a vulnerability there that reassured her more than words ever could. If he was willing to take the risk, so was she. Her legs trembling, she slid her hands up to cup his face. "You think you're the only one with control issues, Rafe Diaz?"

He inched his head back to gaze down at her. "*You* have control issues?"

"Damn right. I love you. I didn't want to. *Don't* want to. But I do."

Gently, he pressed a kiss to her temple. "Think maybe fate took a hand in this?"

"Maybe." She smiled up at him. "It's for sure each of us had our futures mapped out, or so we thought."

"Want to agree to let go of the reins and hold on to each other instead? Let fate take us where it will."

"Together." She lifted her head, found his mouth waiting. "As long as we're together."

"Forever."

Epilogue

The bride was stunning—tall and regal in white lace, her face luminous in the dazzling glow of crystal chandeliers as she danced with the man who was now her husband.

As it had been two months ago for the silent auction, the luxury hotel's ballroom was filled with light, food and flowers. Champagne flowed freely. Dozens of chairs had been arranged in corners and along the art-covered walls. The terrace doors were thrown open to allow the guests to spill out into the crisp fall night.

It didn't take long to change lives, Rafe mused while watching the newlyweds sway together to the soft music. A few moments, a few words.

"Liz and Sam look so happy," Allie said beside him. "It was a beautiful wedding."

Rafe gazed down at the woman who'd played a major hand in changing his life. Twice. Her gold hair fell in soft curls to her shoulders. Her long, rose-colored dress flowed around her. He felt a longing so deep, so intense, he could barely keep from reaching for her.

Later, he promised himself.

"A gorgeous wedding," Claire Castle agreed. Her dress matched Allie's, except for its misty blue color. She smiled up at her tuxedo-clad husband. "I guess all weddings are gorgeous in their own way."

"If you say so," Jackson said, meeting his wife's gaze over the rim of a crystal flute.

Rafe took a sip from the one glass of cold, frothy champagne he'd allowed himself. "It's the first wedding I've been to where the bride almost raced down the aisle to get to the altar."

"You caught that, did you?" Allie asked, grinning. "Liz was engaged before. She never could force herself to walk down the aisle and marry the guy. I think tonight she was determined to get to the front of the church as fast as her legs would take her."

"They look so happy." Claire's voice shook as she gestured her glass of ice water toward the dance floor. "So in love."

Rafe spotted the tears in Claire's eyes at the same instant Allie gripped her friend's hand. "Claire, what is it?" Allie asked.

"Nothing." She sniffed. "I'm just so… Oh, I wasn't going to say anything. Yet."

"Now you've done it," Jackson said softly as he slipped his arm around his wife's waist. "Shall I spill the rest of the beans, or do you want to?"

"What beans?" Allie asked.

Claire gripped her friend's hand. "We didn't want to take any attention away from Sam and Liz, so we planned to wait until they left on their honeymoon to make our announcement. But I just can't hold it in any longer. We're going to have a baby!"

While the women who were as close as sisters embraced, Rafe shook Jackson's hand. "Congratulations."

"Thanks." Jackson gazed at his wife, his eyes filled with an emotion that months ago had been foreign to Rafe.

But Rafe had recently discovered something. He understood now what put that bedazzled look in Jackson Castle's and Sam Broussard's eyes when they looked at the women they loved. Rafe now knew what caused a man to fall so deeply in love it never ended.

It was finding the unique woman, and what knowing her could do to your heart.

He had found that woman, and tonight he was taking the big plunge. He had a diamond ring in his pocket and champagne chilling at home. Just like Jackson and Claire, he'd planned to wait until the newlyweds left to propose.

But he had the ring, and there was enough champagne flowing around them to fill a swimming pool. No time like the present, he decided.

Linking his fingers with Allie's, he leaned closer. "Want to step out onto the terrace with me?"

She sent him a sassy, under-the-lashes look. "Are you going to make it worth my while if I do?"

"I'm going to try." He pressed a kiss against her knuckles. "For the rest of my life, I'm going to try."

* * * * *

Harlequin is 60 years old,
and Harlequin Blaze is celebrating!
After all, a lot can happen in 60 years,
or 60 minutes…or 60 seconds!
Find out what's going down in Blaze's
heart-stopping new miniseries,
FROM 0 TO 60!
Getting from "Hello" to "How was it?"
can happen fast….

Here's a sneak peek of the first book,
A LONG, HARD RIDE
by Alison Kent
Available March 2009.

"Is that for me?" Trey asked.

Cardin Worth cocked her head to the side and considered how much better the day already seemed. "Good morning to you, too."

When she didn't hold out the second cup of coffee for him to take, he came closer. She sipped from her heavy white mug, hiding her grin and her giddy rush of nerves behind it.

But when he stopped in front of her, she made the mistake of lowering her gaze from his face to the exposed strip of his chest. It was either give him his cup of coffee or bury her nose against him and breathe in. She remembered so clearly how he smelled. How he tasted.

She gave him his coffee.

After taking a quick gulp, he smiled and said, "Good morning, Cardin. I hope the floor wasn't too hard for you."

The hardness of the floor hadn't been the problem. She shook her head. "Are you kidding? I slept like a baby, swaddled in my sleeping bag."

"In my sleeping bag, you mean."

If he wanted to get technical, yeah. "Thanks for the loaner. It made sleeping on the floor almost bearable." As had the warmth of his spooned body, she thought, then quickly changed the subject. "I saw you have a loaf of bread and some eggs. Would you like me to cook breakfast?"

He lowered his coffee mug slowly, his gaze as warm as the sun on her shoulders, as the ceramic heating her hands. "I didn't bring you out here to wait on me."

"You didn't bring me out here at all. I volunteered to come."

"To help me get ready for the race. Not to serve me."

"It's just breakfast, Trey. And coffee." Even if last night it had been more. Even if the way he was looking at her made her want to climb back into that sleeping bag. "I work much better when my stomach's not growling. I thought it might be the same for you."

"It is, but I'll cook. You made the coffee."

"That's because I can't work at all without caffeine."

"If I'd known that, I would've put on a pot as soon I got up."

"What time *did* you get up?" Judging by the sun's position, she swore it couldn't be any later than seven now. And, yeah, they'd agreed to start working at six.

"Maybe four?" he guessed, giving her a lazy smile.

"But it was almost two…" She let the sentence dangle, finishing the thought privately. She was quite sure he knew exactly what time they'd finally fallen asleep after he'd made love to her.

The question facing her now was where did this relationship—if you could even call it *that*—go from here?

* * * * *

Cardin and Trey are about to find out that
great sex is only the beginning....
Don't miss the fireworks!
Get ready for
A LONG, HARD RIDE
by Alison Kent
Available March 2009,
wherever Blaze books are sold.

CELEBRATE
60 YEARS
OF PURE READING PLEASURE
WITH HARLEQUIN®!

We'll be spotlighting a different series
every month throughout 2009
to celebrate our 60th anniversary.

Look for Harlequin® Blaze™ in March!

0-60

*After all, a lot can happen in 60 years,
or 60 minutes...or 60 seconds!*

Find out what's going down in Blaze's
heart-stopping new miniseries *0-60!*
Getting from "Hello" to "How was it?"
can happen fast....

Look for the brand-new 0-60 miniseries in March 2009!

Silhouette® Desire

BRENDA JACKSON

TALL, DARK... WESTMORELAND!

Olivia Jeffries got a taste of the wild and reckless when she met a handsome stranger at a masquerade ball. In the morning she discovered her new lover was Reginald Westmoreland, her father's most-hated rival. Now Reggie will stop at nothing to get Olivia back in his bed.

Available March 2009 wherever books are sold.

Always Powerful, Passionate and Provocative.

REQUEST YOUR FREE BOOKS!

2 FREE NOVELS PLUS 2 FREE GIFTS!

Silhouette® Romantic

SUSPENSE

Sparked by Danger, Fueled by Passion!

You're invited to join our Tell Harlequin Reader Panel!

By joining our new reader panel you will:

- Receive Harlequin® books—they are FREE and yours to keep with no obligation to purchase anything!
- Participate in fun online surveys
- Exchange opinions and ideas with women just like you
- Have a say in our new book ideas and help us publish the best in women's fiction

In addition, you will have a chance to win great prizes and receive special gifts! See Web site for details. Some conditions apply. Space is limited.

To join, visit us at
www.TellHarlequin.com.

Silhouette®
Romantic
SUSPENSE

COMING NEXT MONTH

Available February 24, 2009

#1551 THE RANCHER BODYGUARD—Carla Cassidy
Wild West Bodyguards
Grace Covington's stepfather has been murdered, her teenage sister the only suspect. Convinced of her sister's innocence, Grace turns to her ex-boyfriend, attorney Charlie Black, to help her find the truth. Although she's determined not to forgive his betrayal, the sexual tension instantly returns as their investigation leads them into danger...and back into each other's arms.

#1552 CLAIMED BY THE SECRET AGENT—Lyn Stone
Special Ops
COMPASS agent Grant Tyndal was supposed to be on a mission to rescue a kidnapping victim, but Marie Beauclair doesn't need rescuing. An undercover CIA operative, she's perfectly able to save herself. As they work together to catch the kidnapper, will the high-intensity situations turn their high-voltage passion into something more?

#1553 SAFE BY HIS SIDE—Linda Conrad
The Safekeepers
When someone begins stalking a child star, Ethan Ryan is the perfect man to be her bodyguard. But the child's guardian, Blythe Cooper, wants nothing to do with him. As the stalker closes in, sparks fly between Ethan and Blythe, and they soon find their lives—and their hearts—at risk.

#1554 SUSPECT LOVER—Stephanie Doyle
They both wanted a family, so Caroline Sommerville and Dominic Santos agreed to a marriage of convenience. Neither expected love—until it happened. But when Dominic's business partner is murdered, he's the prime suspect and goes on the run. Can Caroline trust this man who lied about his past—the man she now calls her husband?